Nowhere to Go

By

Margaret Ghilchik

Table of Content

Dedications

For Leo Ghilchik

Acknowledgements

Cover illustrations by Golrokh Broumandi

About the Author

Margaret Ghilchik is a writer, a doctor, surgeon, as well as a mother of four and a grandmother of four.

She is the author of a book telling the *Lives* of the first 200 pioneering women doctors who broke through barriers to become Fellows of the Royal College of Surgeons of England, FRCS, *The Fellowship of Women*. The book is a tribute to their courage, resilience, and the evolving role of women in medicine.

Margaret lives on the edge of Hampstead Heath, where she enjoys daily walks with her dog—an enduring source of joy and reflection. In the years following her official retirement, Margaret continued to work across the country, offering her specialist skills and extensive experience. Her contributions remained appreciated and warmly received, and she took great satisfaction in continuing to serve the profession she loved.

Following the COVID-19 pandemic, her long and distinguished surgical career came to a close. Rather than dwell on its ending, she redirected her energy toward new creative pursuits. With characteristic focus and curiosity, she embraced fresh challenges— enrolling in online courses, one of which led to the creation of *Spike*, and turning her attention to manuscripts she had set aside in earlier years.

Chapter 1

Disaster

There was nothing in that beautiful Saturday to give any warning that disaster lay ahead.

Nothing to alert us.

Saturday afternoon is Games for us at the end of the school week. It had been a lovely day, warm with early spring sunshine, no rain. By four o'clock, the afternoon light was just beginning to fade. We were all coming back into school at the end of the day, some boys covered with mud from the rugger field, others almost as muddy, though not quite so boisterous, returning from the hockey pitch, carrying their sticks, tapping the ball between them.

For those of us not in a team, it was Cross-Country. It's not competitive, and I like running at my own pace, threading through the trees in the wood. We come back into the grounds in ones and twos. There are always a few at the end who have slowed from a run to a walk. I did a little extra loop round the front of the school to see the stragglers home.

Our Housemaster had once asked me to check, and ever since I had felt responsible and given him a nod when all were in. He would sometimes acknowledge that with a return nod.

We kicked off our boots, caked with leaves, stacked them into the Boot Room, put some into lockers, and went to shower.

The word had gone round that the Housemaster wanted to have a few words with us once we were washed and down to tea. We thought no more about it, attached no particular significance to the statement.

Saturday evening supper is a casual affair: soup from a great tureen with baguettes, then salad things, tomatoes and cold meats, plates of ham, cold chicken, bread and butter if wanted, in order to give the cooks an evening off. A big bowl of fruit for pudding.

Mr Benson, our Housemaster, was waiting until we had all eaten before telling us what was on his mind. He pushed back his chair and went to stand at the Head of Top Table. He had slipped his arms into his black schoolteacher's gown.

It was unusual for him to wear a gown on a Saturday evening. It was never formal. He tapped a glass with his fork to get our attention. We silenced and turned our faces towards him. He was holding a fistful of small prompt cards for his words. He cleared his throat.

'The Headmaster has asked me to read you this message.'

All heads turned towards him. This was a surprise. He paused and cleared his throat.

'The virus epidemic has continued to spread over the country, and the Government has decided to put the whole country into lockdown in order to limit the spread of infection.'

He spoke slowly to emphasise his words.

'All schools are to close. Ranford School will close by Monday evening. The Headmaster and I both hope that this will not last for too long and we will see you all back in school once it is over.'

We were stunned into silence. He paused and pushed his hair back from his forehead. He shuffled to the next card and then went on.

'Over the next few weeks – it may be months even – we will be connecting with you all through online teaching, and we will expect you to keep regular hours. So take your laptop computers home with you and be ready to connect up. Take your personal things.

Matron, and Ruth and Mary, will be available tomorrow and Monday all day to advise what to pack and what to take. Take as much as possible, I gather, as school will be having a deep clean once we are all departed.'

He consulted the final card in his hand.

'Your parents have been informed and will be expecting you. Boys with parents from overseas will go to their usual contacts here.

They will not be able to stay in school as they usually can in the holidays. There will be no exceptions. School is closing.

Now: coaches will be leaving from the Main Gates to connect with the trains after lunch on Monday. You will all go to your homes on Monday afternoon. The Headmaster and I both hope that this will prove to be a temporary change and we will see you all back in school just as soon as it is over.'

He hunched his shoulders, took his seat again, and folded his arms. There was a stunned silence.

I happened to be at his table; we could sit anywhere on Saturday evening.

We could see he was clearly upset by having to make this announcement. His hand, thrusting the cards back into his inside jacket pocket, was practically shaking.

'Does that mean you too, Sir?' I asked him. 'Do you have to go?'

'It does. The Head has told us all to go. Ranford School is to close. You know, this School House is my home. Just as it is for all you boys. Only even more so. I don't have another house to go to. I will go to my sister's, in fact, in the Highlands of Scotland. It's our family home.'

The Highlands. It was on the tip of my tongue to ask him if I could go along with him, and remind him that I, like him, had no other home to go to.

Before I could ask or say anything, Mr Benson shrugged and went on, 'And unfortunately, my sister is none too happy to have me descend on her for what sounds like an open-ended stay. She is used to having the place to herself. She's an artist, and she spreads her things all around. But it is our family home, mine as well as hers, so I shall go there. I've nowhere else to go.'

Well, that was my Housemaster – and he had nowhere to go! Disaster!

I didn't expect the Housemaster to remember, but it was the same for me. I too had nowhere else to go.

How it came about that I had nowhere to go is quite a story.

My father would describe himself at the moment as a *Guest of Her Majesty*. This was his witty way of saying that he was in prison. He had been given four years, and he had only fairly recently started to serve the sentence because before that there had been the Trial and the Appeal and Waiting. Lots of Waiting.

My father, I knew, was a very clever man. Lively. Like quicksilver. I had been brought up in the home of his parents, my father's parents, Pat and Tony, and they were as solid and dependable as my father was lively.

My father called his parents 'Pat' and 'Tony', rather than Mother and Father. Not *Mother and Father*. Never *Mum and Dad*. So I did too. Called them Pat and Tony. My father flitted in and out of their home—Pat and Tony's house—like a ray of sunshine, a spark of lightning, never staying long. We never knew when he was coming, bringing a few days of excitement, and then he was gone again.

Two or three years ago, Pat had become ill. She got cancer, and slowly it got worse and worse. Tony, her husband, was devastated and increasingly felt he couldn't cope with anything else but looking after her. It was then that my father hit on the idea of sending me to Ranford School. He felt his son would be secure in the school until he was released from prison. Well, he couldn't have anticipated an epidemic that would close all schools.

He had taken me along to see the Headmaster and arranged everything.

The day we met the Headmaster is fixed forever in my mind— for that was the last time I saw my father.

'Pat, I want him dressed in his school blazer. White shirt. School tie. Hair brushed,' my father had said. 'Long grey socks.' I was still in short trousers, though I should have been out of them long before.

My father had no car at that time, but he got a friend to drive us there. We sat in the back of a really swish car on plush leather seats. The friends my father had!

We cruised through the Main Gates and right up to the front doors of the school, the car tyres spurting gravel as we drove into the driveway. My father and I got out. The driver friend stayed put, looking forward.

My father had special words for me; he put his hand firmly on my shoulder.

'Stand up straight, Sebastian. Shake hands with the Headmaster. Call him *Sir*!'

The Headmaster seemed to expect this.

He announced that his wife would take the lad in a moment to his study for him to do a little test.

'Have you got a pen and pencil?' he asked me.

I flipped open my blazer to show him the inner pocket where Pat had put a six-inch plastic ruler, a pencil with a rubber on one end, and my pen.

The Headmaster smiled and inclined his head.

'You have already passed the first part of the test,' he said.

He sat himself down at his desk and my father and I stood before him.

'Now let us get down the particulars. Full name?'

My father said it slowly so that the Headmaster could write it down:

'Sebastian… Peregrine… Kingswell…' – and then my father's surname.

The Head wrote the first three names. He paused and looked up at my father. Straight in the eye, as my father always told me to look at people.

'I think we'll stop at *Kingswell*,' he said. 'Your surname is going to be notorious and all over the papers. Your son has to live in the school. You know what boys can be like.' He emphasised the full stop after *Kingswell* with a dot of his pencil. 'Are we agreed?'

My father nodded. Two or three little nods, up and down, his lips pursed.'So. S.P.K. The boys will make something of that, I expect.' He paused a bit, thoughtfully, tapping his pencil again on the paper, then went on. 'Mother's name?'

I chimed up, 'I have no mother. She didn't want me.'

My father laid a gentle hand on mine.

'Kingswell,' he said, and ducked his head and added a forename softly into the Headmaster's ear.

So that is how I entered the school. Sebastian Peregrine Kingswell. And once the boys heard my name and saw my initials—S.P.K.—they called me *Spike*, and so I was known.

While I went and sat writing the small test in the Headmaster's study, my father went to collect something from the car, and he and the driver friend paid all the fees up front to the Bursar.

The school gave us lunch—sat us down, my father and me, at the end of a long table where we could see some boys further down, chattering away and ignoring us. We had fish with a sauce and mashed potato, a large glass of water, then semolina with a big blob of red jam. All good food. I ate the lot, as did my father, and polished our plates.

The Headmaster's wife, Mrs Clarke, bustled in to collect us. She had a big smile for me.

'You have passed the test, Sebastian,' she said, 'which is Good News.'

She made it sound like a matter for congratulations. *Good News* in capital letters.

'The Headmaster has suggested Mr Benson's House as the most suitable House for you.' She turned to my father. 'Mr Benson is a new young Housemaster and he runs his House in an exceedingly friendly way. I think your son will be very happy there. Would you like to come and visit the House now? Or perhaps, because next week is half-term week, maybe—come and see us when you drop him off Monday week?'

Previous words must have gone over my head, if indeed they had been spoken, because I certainly hadn't focused on the immediacy of my joining the school.

She produced a list of clothing and gear that a boy would need as he entered the school.

'The uniform is quite casual: blazer with school crest, sports jacket, long trousers,' she glanced at my bare knees, 'non-iron white shirts, a couple of ties, school sweater, school socks, vests and pants, pyjamas, lots of sports gear.'

The paper sheets of instructions that she handed over crumpled in my father's hand, and I saw him give his enchanting smile and turn his charm in full splendour on to the Headmaster's wife. He dropped his voice a little and spoke confidingly, his head on one side.

'I wonder if you have someone in school who would be able to help me with this? I have deposited enough for any such contingencies.' He smiled ruefully. He made it sound a little hesitant. 'I fear I myself will not be able to deal with this list. I am on my own with my son. My parents are elderly and my mother in particular has been quite sick,' and he dropped his voice a little further, 'and I am afraid I am due in Court next week.'

I did not know then, but I heard later that the Headmaster's wife was a J.P.—a Justice of the Peace—that is, a judge of sorts. And, without in any way falling for my father's charm, she did understand exactly his predicament about having to attend at Court.

'Leave it with me!' she said in commanding tones, taking the crumpled clothing list off him. 'Sebastian, I think come and see your new House with me. If you stay now, you will have the quiet of the half-term week to settle in. You won't be on your own—there are always some boys staying over—and we can get you kitted out and ready to get down to your schoolwork the following week. Say goodbye to your father now and let's go and find Mr Benson, your Housemaster.'

My father gave me a great hug and said, 'Do your best!' briskly, and left me. I thought he would have offered the Headmaster's wife a hug too, if it had been appropriate—which even he could see it was not.

The Headmaster's wife and I set out together down the corridor to look for Mr Benson and his House.

That is how I started in at Ranford School, and the Headmaster's wife was right—they had picked a very friendly House for me, which became my home and my family. And that was the last time I saw my father.

Now, two years later, the school was closing—shutting down completely—while the epidemic spread, and I had nowhere to go. My father had thought I would be secure here until the time of his release from prison. But he could not have foreseen the sweep of a virus across the country, the total lockdown, and the school closing in entirety. It was a disaster for me.

I had nowhere to go.

I went through all the possibilities that I could think of. There were not many. Actually, there were none.

During those two years, I hadn't really felt acutely the lack of somewhere to go for the holidays. I had had to work hard—at first to catch up and then to keep up—with the schoolwork. School holiday time without lessons was quite relaxing. I could stay on living in the House. There were always a few of us left behind, boys whose parents worked overseas, and foreigners.

It was quite pleasant. We were few in number. We had the boys' common room all to ourselves, where there was a microwave and a kettle and a toaster. The main meals were all provided, and in addition the staples of bread and butter, milk, and apples were put into the common room kitchen. We had the run of the Library.

I had occasional invitations to join friends' families for a week or two—once even at Christmas. And one Christmas I spent at school with a handful of others also left behind, and we were given a good, though rather formal, time by the Headmaster's wife.

It looked as though, on this occasion, this was not going to be possible.

I hadn't gone back to Tony and Pat at all during those first early years. Tony was fully occupied at first with looking after Pat as she underwent various treatments, and I got used to the idea that I would not be going back to them in the school holidays. Then, inevitably, there came one day when Mr Benson called me in for a man-to-boy chat to give me some special news.

'Spike, we have had a letter from your father's parent, Tony, to tell us that his wife Pat has died.'

I said, 'Oh. I know she was very poorly.'

The news was not felt by me as a disaster. I hadn't seen them for over a year. Yes, they were my childhood. But my childhood was past, over and gone.

He said, 'It doesn't seem as though you're expected to go to her funeral. I think it would be a good thing if you were to write a short note to Tony to say how sorry you were. Would you like to do that now in my study and get it over with? Or do you want to think it through?'

'I'll do it now. Thank you, Mr Benson.'

He had school writing paper laid out ready for me at his desk.

'Good man!' said Mr Benson when I had it done. 'It seems to have knocked Tony for six—first looking after her and then losing her. He writes that he doesn't feel able to have you back home or to look after you again. I felt I should let you know that. I was a bit taken aback how strongly he expressed himself.'

I thought that through. I wasn't overly upset myself. I explained to Mr Benson what I thought.

'I think Tony had always thought it was all a bit much—that my father expected them to look after me while he went off and lived his life. Not Pat so much. She was happy to have me to look after. They were very responsible people. And kind to me. And correct.'

I didn't tell Mr Benson that I had a memory—on one occasion, when I was very young, maybe not even three yet, certainly quite young, definitely on my feet though, but perhaps only just, and still difficult to handle as many toddlers are, not amenable to reason. Pat and Tony had read somewhere that a small child needed to see his mother. They didn't tell my father, but took me to see this girl—a teenager, really—and it was a disaster. I think Tony hoped it would give Pat a break, but it was no good trying to repeat that. They were stuck with me.

Anyway, from the point of view of my having somewhere to go, now that school was closing, Tony had made it clear—and even put it in writing to the school—that he was unwilling to look after me again. So, not with him.

I didn't imagine either that my father would get Compassionate Leave from prison to look after me. Like a First World War soldier we had read about in History, they called it *Blighty*. Leave was sometimes granted, sometimes not.

No. I had nowhere to go. I thrashed around in my mind.

Nowhere to go…

UNLESS...

Another conversation with my Housemaster came back to me. I've forgotten what we were talking about—perhaps it was after Tony's letter of rejection of me—but I remembered him saying:

'We all have two sets of grandparents, so two grandfathers. One on your father's side—this one who has written that he is not in a position to take on any more care of you again—and one on your mother's side. Actually, Spike, the Kingswell name is quite well known,' he said. 'He is an authority. On education. On the history of education over the years. You could look his name up in the Library, Spike. He has written books on the influence of the development of education over time. I have read one. It was on our syllabus when I was studying as an undergraduate.'

Then he added, 'Although from what I hear, he himself is quite eccentric and a bit of a recluse.'

I had gone and looked him up—out of interest. I was quite used to using the Library, because it was one thing to do in the holidays when I was marooned in school.

There was a rather dry account of his books and work, and I had noted his address in North London. It stood out because it was an odd one: Hamilton Terrace. Like Lady Hamilton, I thought. Nelson's lady.

So here was one possibility.

I was homeless. With nowhere to go. I would give it a try—first of all, living as a homeless person on my own in London—and see how I got on. It might be alright. I wouldn't know until I tried it.

Then, should things not work out, I would compose a letter to the reclusive, the eccentric, alternative grandfather—if he was indeed a grandfather—and see if he would take me in.

I laid my plan.

I would simply take the coach to the station with all the other boys, mingling, saying nothing. They were all busy packing up their gear. I did the same. I made an additional emergency bag of torch, notepad and pencil, spare warm clothing, together with my laptop, and strapped my sleeping bag to the top of my backpack. My plan was to take the train to London along with all the others.

Then, I knew where I would go in London.

I would make my way first to Lincoln's Inn Fields and try and see how I would manage with sleeping out. As a homeless person. Just in case. Because that's what I was—homeless.

We had visited the museum in Lincoln's Inn Fields once with the school, and there had been a van there, parked on the corner, with *Soup for the Homeless* painted on its side. We had had a joke that some of us would queue up for free soup and see if we could sample it, but of course we didn't do it.

This time, that's what I would be when school closed on Monday: homeless.

We had heard that there had been campers there in the past, pitching their tents on the grass under the trees in the Square. I would give it a try for at least a night—sleeping rough—and see how I got on with it. It might be alright. I might try busking—singing at the bottom of the escalators in Holborn tube station, the longest escalators in the Tube, I think—seeing if I could earn a few pennies.

But then, if I didn't feel I could go along with it and continue, I would write a letter to this Grandfather Kingswell and put it through the letterbox of his house in Hamilton Terrace, and see if he would let me stay.

I checked his address again in the Library. John, he was called. John Kingswell. So, Grandfather John.

I began to work out what I wanted to say in the letter.

Chapter 2

Letter to Grandfather

Dear Grandfather John,

I am writing to you because I urgently need your help. School has closed down and we are all being sent home because of the virus epidemic. I have a big problem: I cannot go home. I have nowhere to go. Most boys will go home to their parents. I cannot be sent to live with mine. Unfortunately, that is quite impossible.

My father is serving his four-year sentence for fraud, though he fortunately managed to pay my school fees in advance before he went down, and probably has more squirreled away for when he comes out. He thought I would be secure to stay in school until he is released. But now it seems that is not so. He could not have known that a virus epidemic would sweep the country and the school close down entirely.

I asked my Housemaster if I could stay at school, as I normally would during the school vacation. I said I would be very quiet and no trouble at all, but he is going up to Scotland where he has a sister, and will stay with her. Like me, he has no home apart from his

Housemaster's house. His sister's place is in the Highlands and sounds just the sort of place to be in during these troubled times. I couldn't really expect him to take me along—though I might ask again if staying with you is any problem.

School has been wonderful for me. School is my family, my home. I cannot believe that they can just close it down and cast me out. I have wondered if I could sneak back into school and hide out there. Then I thought I would see if I could manage to live outside for a bit, as a homeless person. I have got all my gear in my backpack and a sleeping bag. I fear it may prove to be more difficult than I anticipate, but I will give it a try for the first night and see how I get on.

I am going to Lincoln's Inn Fields. I will have some soup from the van that parks there for the homeless. I saw it stationed on the corner when we went to visit the museum. The soup will be warming, at least. There is a place to sit in an entry down the steps by the museum that I thought might be secure, but not if there are ashes and coal dust by the dustbins. I think I may be better off in the gardens of the Square. They lock the gates at night, but I imagine it should not be too difficult to get in if I throw my things over—sleeping bag and backpack—and climb in after them.

I plan to find a good spot and dig into my backpack for an extra sweater and trousers, and pull them on over my other clothes to feel better protected from the cold, then climb into my sleeping bag. The shrubs and trees of the Square cast shadows, so I should not be spotted. I am not afraid. At midnight they extinguish the streetlights around the Square and I will lie on my back and gaze at the familiar stars, like diamonds in the clear night sky. I really want to see if I can manage to sleep out on my own.

The next morning, my plan is to see if I can earn some money busking at Holborn–Kingsway Tube station, which is nearby. It has the longest escalator, and I plan to set up at the bottom of it and play a plaintive tune. Maybe *The Londonderry Air* or *The boy to the wars has gone, in the ranks of death you'll find him*. That's how I am beginning to feel—rather resigned and bereft.

I realise too that even if I manage living as a homeless person, it would be difficult, maybe impossible, to connect up with the lessons that school is meant to be streaming online to all boys.

Then, Grandpa John, the day after my night under the stars, I plan to put this letter through your letterbox and give you time to read it and think about it. Then I will come and sit on your doorstep and see if you will take me in and put me up until school starts again.

My Housemaster says you are an authority, and one of your books was on his syllabus when he was at university. He said he had heard that you may be a recluse and estranged from family—but anyway, we have not met, so you cannot be estranged from me.

In case you have forgotten me, I am Sebastian Peregrine Kingswell—S.P.K.—not my choice of names, but the initials mean that I am called Spike by my friends.

Respectfully yours,

Spike

Chapter 3

Homeless

I did quite well at sleeping under the stars. There was no one about when I hurled my sleeping bag over the fence and gently dropped my backpack after it. Climbing in was less easy. I managed it only with some difficulty—otherwise, I would really have been in a pickle, with my gear on one side and myself on the other.

I found a good grassy area to settle down where I wouldn't be spotted, sheltered by trees and bushes. I dug out extra clothes to put on until I looked like a Michelin Man and wriggled into the sleeping bag. It was surprisingly uncomfortable.

At first, I sat up in the sleeping bag, reading what I had written by the light of my small torch, which shone a pool of light onto the notepad I balanced on my knees. The pencil, writing pad, and small torch were all part of the escape kit that I had assembled in my backpack. I could hardly see in the dim light to read through all the words, but I would read them again in the morning once daylight came.

Carefully, I detached the pages from the pad, folded them, and returned the letter, notepad, and pencil back into my bag. I switched off the torch—it was important to conserve the battery—and stowed it safely away, then zipped the bag shut. The backpack made a rather lumpy pillow, but at least it was secure while it was under my head. I snuggled down into the sleeping bag and pulled it tightly around me.

I looked up at the night sky. It was a clear, cloudless night—no rain—and I could see the stars studded across the sky: Orion and his belt, and further over, the saucepan shape of the Great Bear and the Pole Star, reassuringly watching over me. I didn't think I would easily get off to sleep, listening to the rustling in the shrubs and trees of the Square. It was different being here on my own. But I did. Long before they switched the streetlights off, I was already asleep—and I slept quite soundly.

I was woken none too gently by the thrust of a boot giving my sleeping bag a good kick or two, and a gruff voice saying,

'Now then, now then! You can't doss down here.'

I came to and woke up very fast, sitting up in my sleeping bag. I found I was looking into the weathered old face of the gardener or caretaker of the Square Gardens. I climbed out of my bag and stood up.

'Good gracious! You're just a child!' the old man said. 'Now look you here, I've unlocked the gates to the Square and opened up the public conveniences, so get and use the Gents, then take yourself off.'

I began to do as I was told—folded my sleeping bag into a roll and secured it with a strap, tucking it under one arm, and hoisted my backpack onto the other shoulder as the caretaker stood and watched me. I set off across the Square in the direction indicated by the old man's thumb, to the featureless cement building.

He shouted after me,

'And don't come back here tomorrow. This is no place for a boy to be sleeping.'

Once there, I found I could get organised. There was no one else inside. I took off the Michelin Man extra sweater and trousers I'd put on for further warmth, stowed them away, and fastened my sleeping bag securely onto the top of the knapsack. I splashed water from the basin onto my face and gave my hands and face a good, refreshing wash. I was ready to go.

To my surprise, the soup-for-the-homeless van was driving back into the Square to take up its position on the corner. Already one or two stragglers were ambling toward it. I followed after one old tramp of a fellow and, like him, I was given a bacon butty and a cardboard mug of tea—which was very welcome. I took it to a nearby bench and sat to eat and drink.

I got out my letter and read what I had written. It was too late to change it, but it did say exactly what I needed it to say.

I didn't have much joy busking at the foot of the escalators. A few coins were tossed onto my backpack before the station staff descended on me like a fury and made it clear that one needed to be the possessor of a licence to play or sing for money.

I set off for my grandfather's house in Maida Vale. I had the address—Hamilton Terrace—and strode off, walking to make my way there. I did wonder if I might have been taken there to visit in my childhood, but when I got there—definitely not. I had no recollection of ever having been there before.

Grandfather's house was a tall building, one in a terrace of similar houses. The front gardens were paved behind a low front wall and were mainly occupied by Council dustbins. Though at my grandfather's, a wisteria clambered up over the porch—the fronded pale green leaves hanging gracefully, covering the pillars and promising glorious bluey-mauve blossoms later.

Grandfather seemed to own the whole house; there were none of those little name cards and bells that indicated the house had been divided up into multiple flats. There was just the one large bow window to the right of the front door, and I imagined that this might be Grandfather's study. Perhaps he was sitting there even now, and would shortly be reading the letter in which I introduced myself.

I wondered what he would look like. Was he old? And bearded? With a kind old face? Wrinkled? Bespectacled? Stern? Would he be friendly?

I went through the open gateway and deposited my backpack just inside the low wall. I took out the letter and approached the front door, stepped up into the porch, and posted it through the letterbox. I could feel my heart thumping with anxiety. The letterbox closed with a metallic clunk. No dog barked from inside. I heard no sound of footsteps coming to see what the postman had brought. The warm, sweet smell of the wisteria filled the air.

I went and sat on the wall next to my backpack to wait. It seemed a long time since the bacon butty and cardboard mug of tea. I slid down onto the ground, leaned back against the wall, shut my eyes, and dozed off.

I was alerted by the sound of the front door opening, footsteps, and the door closing with a bang. A stout, middle-aged woman had let herself out. I got to my feet. I had not expected a woman to come out, but I recognised at once who she would be.

She looked a lot like the women who served the meals in the House at school—women who also did our washing and kept the communal areas of the House clean and in order. We schoolboys addressed them by their first names, in a friendly fashion—Ruth, and Mary—and they worked under the benevolent rule of Matron. They were part of the school family as I regarded them. So, this was not Grandfather's wife. Or lady friend. Or so I judged.

I stepped forward.

'Hello,' I said. 'I'm Mr Kingswell's grandson. Is he in? May I come in?'

She looked at me suspiciously.

'I'm not aware he has a grandson,' she said. She spoke with a slight accent. 'Is he expecting you?'

'I've put my letter through the door introducing myself,' I said.

'So, he doesn't know you're coming then,' she said. 'You'd better wait here until I've spoken to him.'

And she went back in, letting herself in with her key and shutting the door. She was a long time inside. After a while, I slid down again and sat on the ground just inside the wall.

I thought to myself, *I hope they are reading my letter.*

As time dragged on, an unwelcome thought crossed my mind. Doubt troubled me. How sure was I that this Kingswell was my grandfather? I tried to recollect what my Housemaster had actually said, but the exact words escaped me. Had he just said someone of the same name? *A recluse*—I remembered that. *An academic who had written a book.* I thrust the unwelcome thoughts out of my mind.

At last, she reappeared. Her attitude had not changed one bit. She was still clearly suspicious of me and unhappy about admitting me.

'I'm Mrs Robinson,' she said. 'I do for Mr Kingswell. I have to say, I've never heard that he had a grandson. You won't mind me asking—have you any identity?'

I thought, what sort of identity could I have? I did have a passport, but it was secure in the Headmaster's office. I was too young to have a driving licence. Well, I had a library card. That had my name on it. I fished it out of my jacket pocket.

'I'm a schoolboy,' I said. 'From Ranford School.'

'Well, you'll have to wait. He's still in his dressing gown and I've suggested he gets up. He's quite old and absent-minded. And I'll wait around and see everything's above board.'

She looked at the library card and wasn't much reassured by my explanation of what it was and that it had my name on it.

'Why would you bring a library card?' she said. 'This isn't a library.'

'Of course not,' I said, feeling that I had not made things much better. 'But it has my name on it—Sebastian Kingswell. Which is a sort of identity.'

She snorted.

I decided to throw myself on her mercy. I did feel, after all, that I knew how I should speak to the Mrs Robinsons, or the Ruths or Marys of this world—how to appeal to them.

'Mrs Robinson, I am sorry to trouble you, but I wonder if you could possibly fix me something to eat. I am starving. I've had very little to eat since I left school, and that seems a long time ago.'

It hit the right spot.

'Come with me,' she said, with something that approached the glimmer of a smile. 'There's probably something of Mr Kingswell's breakfast still left.'

And so it was that when Grandfather came down later, he found the grandson he had never met—me—and his housekeeper eating breakfast together around his kitchen table. It nicely broke the ice.

Mrs Robinson got up at once and insisted on fetching a second breakfast before taking herself off, leaving us eating a meal together—than which there is no better bonding experience. She had things to do, she said, shopping to fetch, but she would look in later and see if there was anything he wanted her to do. She seemed reasonably reassured that all was well with the unexpected visitor.

'I have your letter before me,' said my grandfather, indicating the lined paper he set down on the table. 'I am aware that they are closing all schools because of the virus epidemic. But school should surely make proper provision for the boys. What do you normally do in the holidays?' he inquired in a not unfriendly manner.

'I usually get invited by one or other of my friends—boys in the House, or sometimes even boys from other Houses—for part of the time. Sometimes I even get two invites. And then I can also be back in school. There is no problem normally in staying in school for part of the holiday time. It is quite pleasant, actually, being alone in the dormitory. We have study areas, and a common room for boys, and there is always the library. We always have a holiday task to be getting on with and I can work on that. And in fact, we have foreign boys who often stay in the holidays, or boys whose parents work overseas who can't always fly back to them. So the Housemaster still organises food and stuff.'

I took a deep breath.

'But that is not possible now, it seems. School has closed down completely.'

To my embarrassment, I felt tears brimming in my eyes. I covered this stupid weakness by buttering the last piece of toast, smothering it with marmalade, and saying how grateful I was for the meal.

Grandfather was watching me.

'Boys and their appetites!' he said. 'Mrs Robinson is always urging me to eat more. But one loses the sense of hunger as one gets older.'

'I *was* hungry,' I said.

'I was wondering one other thing,' said Grandfather, prodding the letter with his finger. 'What made you pick on Lincoln's Inn Fields?'

'The train from school gets into Waterloo, and there were lots of us boys on the train, of course, travelling. They all knew where they were going—mostly being met. Some were off to a different platform to catch another train, or transferring to another station.

'I did wonder whether it might suddenly occur to someone that I was on my own and insist on taking me along. But I don't imagine it occurred to anyone on this occasion to invite me—with the virus all about. One moment we were all getting off the train onto the platform, and the next moment they had all gone. Gone their different ways.

'I set out walking. It is just a short way to Lincoln's Inn. We visited the museum there on a school trip, and I had noticed the van stationed on the corner providing soup for the homeless. I had my emergency kit in my backpack, and a sleeping bag, and I thought I would see how I could manage.'

We sat in silence for a moment. I was aware that I was not giving an entirely accurate answer to the question of why I had selected Lincoln's Inn Fields. I liked to be truthful. Indeed, I had an almost obsessive dedication to honesty in all things. And whatever the outcome of my request to stay at Grandfather's house, I did not want to be anything but straight and open in my dealings with him.

I felt I must explain what lay behind my selection of the square, but my thinking was becoming muddled. I could not recall all the facts that underlay my choice, and now, suddenly, the words would not come. I felt hot and my face flushed.

Out of the blue, I was struck by extreme tiredness—fatigue such as I had never known before. The room was beginning to swim, and my eyelids were drooping. My head dropped. I realised that I was actually beginning to fall asleep sitting on the chair at the table.

I felt, rather than heard, Grandfather shepherding me from the kitchen into the front room, leading me by holding my upper arm, walking me along, saying,

'Come now. Come now.'

And when I subsided onto the sofa, he put my feet up, a cushion under my head, and covered me over with a travelling rug. I could hear myself keep saying the same words,

'Sorry. Sorry.'

And then I had fallen asleep, and after a bit, I was faintly aware of Mrs Robinson's return and could hear, as through a veil, their conversation and discussion, and then her move to bustle and prepare the spare room for me.

'We'll leave him as he is, on the sofa. Best not to wake him from a sleep like that,' she had said wisely.

'I will sit at my desk. I've got plenty of writing to be getting on with,' Mr Kingswell was speaking. 'And if I get tired, I will put myself into my old leather armchair here, with my feet up on the footstool, and keep watch on him. I shall be fine.' He sounded a bit anxious. 'Do you think he's all right?'

I wanted to speak up and reassure them that I was quite all right, but I was too exhausted to trouble to find the words.

'Don't you worry. He's just worn out with the uncertainty of it all, and lack of proper sleep. Now, you've salad and ham for lunch. There's enough for two. There's a fresh loaf on the breadboard and butter. And there's shepherd's pie to warm up for your supper. There's plenty for you both, should he wake. I'll look in as usual in the morning.'

She paused, and I heard her turn in the doorway.

'And I'm not too concerned about who he is. I can see the family likeness!' she retorted, and with that, she was off, and I heard the click of the door as she went out.

Chapter 4
Grandfather

The day was slipping away by the time I stirred from sleep and sat up. I must have slept a few hours more, but I woke still tired, yet ready to speak and communicate again. As I opened my eyes, I could see through the big bay window that the light was fading. I swung my feet from the sofa onto the floor and sat up.

Grandfather said,

'That's better. Now, take yourself upstairs and have a good shower, wash your hair, and then come down clean to the kitchen.' He was clearly a man who spoke directly.

'You'll find Mrs Robinson has put your things in the spare room,' he went on. 'Have you got a change of clothes?'

I nodded. I had, and I heaved myself unsteadily to my feet and started off toward the stairs before focusing on what he had said about my things being in the spare room. I stopped and asked,

'Grandfather, does that mean that I can stay?'

'We'll have a talk when you come down,' was the uncompromising answer.

There is nothing as good as a hot shower and a hair wash to revive a boy as tired as I was. I used Grandfather's Old English Lavender soap, which lathered copiously, ridding myself of the sweat and grime from the night spent homeless, then rinsed it all off.

Mrs Robinson had put out a fresh towel, and I dried and towelled myself vigorously. In the mirror, I could see dark circles under my eyes and my hair was a mop, but I came down clean and changed into fresh clothes to find Grandfather still in his study, sitting at his desk. I sat down again on the sofa, and Grandfather turned from the desk to speak to me.

'I want you to know,' Grandfather said, 'that I would not have a lot of time to look after you. I am writing a new work, and I spend a lot of time sitting at my desk here or in my chair, thinking, or reading my notes and my reference books. I have written several books, but I do think this one may be the most important yet. I sometimes sit and think for hours, then make a few notes. When my thoughts have come together, I write longhand, often in pencil, here in my exercise books. Then I get them typed up over there at the little desk in the corner, where there is the computer and printer. I don't compose on the computer.'

'That sounds wonderful!' I said. 'That's just how I would like to study and work. We've been told that there will be schoolwork sent to us. I gather I shall have plenty of stuff sent to me from school online to work on, and I have my laptop in my bag.' I looked around the study at the library shelves that flanked the back wall, stuffed with books, and added,

'I shouldn't be short of books!' I looked at the desk where Grandfather sat and wrote his work, then at the other little desk, and voiced my thoughts,

'If there is another little table like that one, where the computer and printer are sitting, I could connect up there. I would be a very quiet presence.'

Grandfather ignored that and said,

'And also, I am old and sometimes need a lot of sleep. Then, other times, when the ideas come thick and fast, I sleep very little and work for hours. I am used to being on my own. Sometimes I don't talk at all for days while I'm working. Mrs Robinson is used to me. I am afraid it would be very dull for you.'

'Grandfather, I won't be dull,' I said. 'And I wouldn't get in your way. Maybe you could just talk to me occasionally while we eat...'

Grandfather clapped a hand to his forehead and leapt to his feet,

'Eat! There you go, you see. I've forgotten already. Mrs Robinson has left us ham and salad and a fresh loaf of bread and butter – and for supper later, there is a shepherd's pie that would need warming up.'

We made our way to the table in the kitchen, and I at once busied myself laying a place for two. Mrs Robinson had made it easy for me, leaving out two large plates for the ham and salad, two smaller ones for the bread and butter, and knives and forks. I set about filling the two tall glasses with water from the tap. I went over to the breadboard, cut two slices of bread, and brought them to the table.

As we sat to eat, I asked him politely,

'Do you want to talk to me about your new book, Grandfather?'

'I will talk about my book and study later on. My work is on education and society, historically, over the years,' he said, 'but first, I think we should clear the decks a bit about the family. Let's start with you, Sebastian, or shall I call you Spike? Tell me about yourself. I don't even know if you have brothers or sisters. I presume not. Nor why you are still a Kingswell and talk about a father—in prison? How was your childhood? How have you got to be where you are now?'

Grandfather laid his knife and fork down across his plate.

'I have had all I want of the ham and salad, and just half that slice of bread and butter will be enough for me, if you'll cut it in two for me. You have what you want.' He sipped his water.

'I will perhaps tell you about your mother, my daughter, and why I think things went wrong for her. That is, when you are ready to hear. And if you would like to hear. But first, you tell me about yourself. Shall I call you Sebastian?'

'I would be glad if you would call me Spike, Grandfather. And it gives me great satisfaction to call you Grandfather. A really secure feeling. I am afraid I am rather an odd boy. My father is a very clever man, but he is a chancer and was arrested for fraud. He is serving a prison sentence. It was in all the newspapers, and when I got a place at Ranford School, both my father and the Headmaster thought I would be better off using Kingswell as a surname. I already had Kingswell as one of my names, so we dropped my father's name.

'When I was a small child, it was his parents, my father's parents, who provided a home for me. They were very nice people – I would say they were good people – and I wanted for nothing. My father came and went. I think he is so clever, my father, and so different from them that they never really understood him; they admired him, but he lived a life outside their compass. He called his parents Pat and Tony, and so I called them the same. When I was very little, they once made an effort for me to see my mother because they felt it was the right thing to do. They tried to send me to visit her, but it was a disaster. She was not interested. I am sure it would have been a nuisance for her to have me to stay, and if there was a stepfather as well, things would have been worse. I don't remember anything about it really, as it was when I was very young, except I do remember refusing ever to go again. I was well off with Pat and Tony, and with my father flitting in from time to time. It was enough. But two years ago, Pat got cancer, and Tony exhausted himself looking after her. It was the time of my father's court case, and Tony kept most of it from Pat while she was ill. That was when my father arranged for me to go to Ranford School. That was the best decision he ever made. The school has been my saviour. It is such a good school, and I am in a very friendly House.'

We were silent for a while as we ate.

'And then?' said Grandfather.

'Well, Pat died. My Housemaster got me to write a short note to Tony when she died. I hadn't seen them at all since I went away to school. School had been enough, really. Then after she died, Tony wrote to school and made it clear that he could no longer be expected to look after me. My Housemaster was a bit taken aback, I think. He thought it had all been too much for Tony – his wife's illness and treatment, then her death, and also all the publicity of their son's case. But they are now part of my past. Maybe Tony feels they were taken advantage of, having me dumped on them. I don't think Pat felt that. They never made me feel unwanted. But I think Tony had had enough and doesn't want the responsibility of me again. They were such good people, Pat and Tony. They didn't deserve such a difficult life or any sadness.'

My grandfather was listening sympathetically to my account.

'I have never met either of them, of course,' he said, 'so it's difficult for me to say. But life can be hard for some people.'

'Well, Grandfather, they were my childhood,' I said. 'And now they are my past.'

'And now?' said Grandfather. 'With school closing. What now?'

I had to add, 'My father is unable to help, as he is in prison.' And then, again, 'But I have been lucky in my school.'

Still, Grandfather said nothing.

We had finished the ham and salad and a slice and a half of bread and butter. I looked at the shepherd's pie.

'Shall we have a taste of Mrs Robinson's pie, Grandfather?' I said.

Grandfather smiled.

'Serve yourself a small portion and heat it in the microwave,' he said. 'You get off to bed when you've had the pie. I think I'll go and sit at my desk in a moment and be there for a little while. I've got more than enough to think about with a grandson who is going to eat me out of house and home. Tomorrow there's a small table on the top landing that can be brought down for you to have your own desk in the study.'

He watched while I served myself a portion of shepherd's pie and put it in the microwave.

'I think three minutes,' I said. 'It looks very good. We have microwaves in the boys' common room, for pot noodles, you know.' I set it in motion. 'Grandfather, while it heats, if you don't mind, I will fetch the small table down from the top landing.' And off I went.

Grandfather sighed. He took himself off to his study and settled himself into his comfortable leather armchair. He could hear me carefully carrying the small table down the stairs. He indicated where it might stand. He announced that he couldn't have carried it down himself.

'The strength of youth!' he sighed.

Later, he said he was gratified to hear noises from the kitchen that indicated I was washing up the dishes.

I popped my head into the study.

'Goodnight, Grandfather.'

'Goodnight, Spike. Sleep well, grandson.'

Well, tomorrow was another day.

Chapter 5

The Headmaster's Wife

When Grandfather came downstairs the next morning, he found me, his grandson, already installed at the second small table, sitting on a chair that I had carried in from the kitchen. I am sure I looked more rested after a good night's sleep. I looked up from the computer and beamed at Grandfather.

'Good morning, Grandfather!' I said. 'The good news is that school has already been in touch with all the boys, and they will be sending out a work programme. I've got connected.'

'Have you had breakfast yet?' he asked.

'I made some toast from the bread on the breadboard – the bread we had yesterday. I hope that's alright. Shall I get you something, Grandfather?' But before he could reply, we heard the click of the front door opening and Mrs Robinson bustled in. She took me off to show me what I could cook, where the pans and saucepans were kept, what was in the larder and what was in the fridge.

'I had some of your shepherd's pie, Mrs Robinson,' I told her. 'Very good indeed. And I put all the food away and washed up the things.'

'Quite right!' she said and called Grandfather in. 'I'm having no nonsense,' she said. 'It will be the making of you to have to eat regular meals. Between the three of us, we shall manage to put some order into this household.'

We sat down obediently to eat the breakfast she was cooking, and Mrs Robinson vanished upstairs to check on the bathroom and bedrooms, leaving them spotless, then a quick dust of the study/sitting room.

Before she left, she fixed Grandfather with a firm look. 'We shall have to come to an arrangement, Mr Kingswell, if you want me to look in more often. And there will be some extra food shopping.'

'Of course,' he said. 'You must tell me whatever… You know I'm not very practical. But I don't expect you to do food shopping and look after us for nothing.'

'Hrrumph!' she said. 'I will let you know.'

And with that, she was gone. Grandfather raised his eyebrows and made a face with his mouth, glimmering a smile at me, and we exchanged glances. He had quite bushy eyebrows over eyes that were a penetrating pale blue. I could see that, like me, he had spruced himself up this morning. Grandfather was wearing a long grey woollen cardigan over his shirt and woollen tie, loosely knotted. The woolly had deep pockets, in one of which he had an ironed, folded handkerchief.

As we poured a final cup of tea, I said to him, 'I will wash up the breakfast things when we've finished, but I just want to put one thing straight. You asked me why I landed up in Lincoln's Inn Fields. I wasn't quite frank about that. The fact is I chose it because last year, I and two other boys from school had a jape there.'

Grandfather raised his eyebrows. 'A jape?'

'It was exeat: we were free from Friday midday – we get a long weekend every few weeks like that – an exeat – and we were not expected back at school until Sunday evening. We thought it would be fun to see what it was like to sleep out in sleeping bags in London. We had heard that they didn't lock the gates to Lincoln's Inn, and it had been invaded by campers, New Zealanders and Australians mostly. They had tents, and rumour had it that postmen brought them their letters; they even had their morning newspaper delivered to them. Like a little colony, apparently. We didn't see that, really, but we did just get in on the end of it before the authorities clamped down on it and evicted them. It was quite fun. They were more or less friendly to us, but they weren't keen on being joined by others. We only stayed two nights, then back to school for Sunday evening. It was quite an adventure. I thought it would be as easy this time, but in fact, they had all gone, the tents all cleared away and the gates locked at night.'

'Did school get to know?' Grandfather asked.

'They did. And they weren't pleased. Two of us got into trouble. They gave us a chore to do. We had to clean the Headmaster's wife's car. I don't think they ever knew we had a third boy with us. Well, they may have guessed because he came to clean the car with us!'

Grandfather chuckled. 'Not much gets past them, I expect.'

Grandfather and I, man and boy, settled down to our respective work places, and actually, we felt there was no reason why life should not continue in a harmonious way. But of course, life is more complicated than that. And it was not to be.

'I suppose sometime I should phone school and let them know that you are here, Spike. Remind me if I haven't done so in a day or two.'

'I don't think there is anyone there,' I said.

'Oh, there will be, a secretary and someone left in charge.'

Indeed there was, and when Grandfather and I phoned a few days later, he reminding himself to say Sebastian and not Spike, the response surprised us. An efficient secretary answered and said she had the file for Sebastian Kingswell before her and in her hands in a minute.

'We have informed Sebastian's father, but he is –' she paused. 'A guest of Her Majesty at the moment, and clearly would be unable to provide him with a home. But we were given an alternative address of a Miss Alicia Kingswell, and we wrote to her.'

'You shouldn't have done that!' said Grandfather sharply. 'She is not a suitable person to receive him.' He whispered to me with his hand over the mouthpiece that he knew he should have spoken with them earlier.

They could hear the secretary taking a sharp breath. 'May I know who you are?' she said. 'We received a phone call from Miss Alicia Kingswell only this morning, and she seemed very gathered and organised, I judged.'

Grandfather shook his head. He could see that he must handle the situation with better diplomacy.

'I am his grandfather,' he said. 'He came to me and has set up his work online in my study and settled in here. If you could give me the contact number for Miss Alicia, it would be helpful. She is my daughter, but as I am sure you know, families can be complicated. I would like to let her know that he is settled here. And perhaps you could tell her that he is going to stay here.'

'I will give you the contact phone number and address for Miss Kingswell in a moment,' she said, 'but first, I would like to speak to Sebastian himself. On his contact card here, it says that his grandfather feels he can no longer be responsible for him.'

'I imagine that is his other grandfather. His father's parents had provided a home for him until recently. Pat and Tony, he called them. Sebastian told me that Pat had died and Tony felt it was all too much for him. That is why he has come to me. He is just standing here next to me while I make this phone call.'

There was a silence on the other end of the phone.

'Nevertheless, I should like to speak with him, if you would put him on the phone.' She sounded determined.

'Of course,' Grandfather said. 'As I said, he is just standing here by me. Spike, the School Secretary would like a word with you.'

'I am the Headmaster's wife, Mr Kingswell, not the school secretary.'

'I am so sorry,' Grandfather said. 'I'm afraid I don't know your name.' Then, hearing it from her, 'Good to talk to you, Mrs Clarke. I will put Sebastian on the line,' and he spoke again to me, 'Spike, the Headmaster's wife would like a word with you. It's Mrs Clarke.'

Grandfather put his hand over the receiver and said to me, 'I should have phoned earlier. I need to speak to her again before we ring off to get a contact number from her.'

He handed over the telephone receiver.

I nodded and proceeded to have a difficult conversation with the Headmaster's wife. She was trying to make me see that the school always needed to know where I was and whether I was safe and secure. She had been able to see that I was connected for receiving the lessons online, but she did not know where I actually was.

'Did you not think to let us know where you were? If you had gone to the house of one of your friends, as you did before in some of the holidays, their parents always phoned to let us know that you were with them.'

Nonchalantly, I tried to insist that I was quite alright.

I realised that I needed to be careful with my answers to cover up the fact that I had spent the first night under the stars.

She persisted, 'Did you not think to phone yourself to let us know where you were?'

'I thought there was no one in school,' I said. 'I thought you had all gone away. I thought that there would be no one there to answer the phone and that it would just ring and ring. I imagined when school was closed, it would be like a ghost town and you had all left. And then when we do come back, there would be dust on the desks and spiders' webs everywhere.' I got carried away with my description. Then I had a further thought. 'There is one thing, Mrs Clarke,' I said. 'Have you got my Housemaster's address and phone number? He went to stay with his sister in Scotland. – Why do I want it? – Well, I just do.'

It did not seem to be forthcoming.

'She'll let me know,' I said at last, as I handed the phone back to Grandfather. 'She wants to ask Mr Benson first.'

Grandfather was given the address and the phone number that he wanted.

The Head's wife still had more to say to us both. Mrs Clarke stated firmly that she had now noted down Grandfather's name, his address, and phone number on her card index, along with his relationship to Sebastian. Sebastian was, after all, a pupil at her school. And the school needed to know – at all times – where their boys were. She said that he was not the only boy in the school with a complicated family history. She advised that, whatever the family circumstances, she thought a boy should be informed that his mother had phoned in after receiving a letter from school. She spoke firmly and with authority:

'My belief is, Mr Kingswell, that it is better not to have any secrets.'

Grandfather thanked her and said he would think it over.

Chapter 6

Alicia

Alicia Kingswell woke slowly, with an overwhelming sense of well-being, as the sun streamed in through the gap in the curtains. She had not felt so brimming with good health in years. Something strange was occurring. She wasn't sure what. She lay for a while contemplating the situation.

No man in the bed beside her. That was one thing. But the change was greater than that. He had gone back to his wife and children now that the virus had descended on the streets. She didn't mind.

She pulled back the heavy curtains—Liberty linen, their prettiest pattern, lined and padded with cotton slub—revealing a glorious sunny day. Warm for spring. Not common in April. But it was more than that. Something unusual had happened.

She sat on the edge of the bed and thrust her feet into her slippers, pulling the little tab at the back of the grey Mahabis soft shoes so they closed snugly around her ankles. She drained the glass of water that always stood on her bedside table in a small crystal glass.

Then it came to her—the thing that was so unusual, so extraordinary. It was her mind. Her mind and her thinking were clear. Crystal clear. Her thoughts were untroubled, not jumping around in a jagged, uncontrolled way, nor lost in a fog.

When she came back from a quick visit to the bathroom, she again sat on the edge of the bed to think. Her mind was razor-sharp, none of the usual muddled confusion. Then it came to her—the explanation for why she was thinking with such clarity now. It came to her in a bound.

The courier who normally brought her drugs had been unable to deliver her habitual dose because of the virus epidemic. This, then, was what it felt like to be without the mind-numbing, dumbing-down effects of narcotics. She was clean.

Should she have a drink to celebrate? No. She would stick to water. She might even have some breakfast.

Shower first. Hairwash and bodywash. Then lather her squeaky-clean hair with conditioner, the lanolin softening the wet locks. Then rinsed. And her body, once dried with a voluminous fluffy towel, was smothered with body creams. She lay on a fresh towel on the bed to allow time for the cream to soak into her skin.

Now her mind was relaxed. Untroubled.

She slipped into her light pale grey cashmere dressing gown and padded to the front door, intending to put the chain on. A long white envelope lay on the mat. How long had it been there, she wondered? She stooped, picked it up, and laid it on the breakfast bar.

Tomorrow, she decided, she would change all the locks. She needed to feel secure. She had every intention of denying access to both the returning partner and the courier. She might need to settle her account with the courier if her partner did not pay, but she could do that with the door opened a crack on the chain.

She wondered how much she owed. She revelled in the range and pliability of her thoughts as she planned how she might organise her life.

She thought she could manage some breakfast, but when it came to it, all she could face was thinly buttered toast and weak tea. She spooned the delicate leaves of Earl Grey into the warmed teapot and let it stand to brew for three minutes before pouring.

The tea and toast lay on the surface of the breakfast bar before her, the tea a watery, clear light brown in a delicate bone china cup with a gold rim and green Chinese dragons chasing each other around the curve. The toast she had cut into four triangles.

She sniffed at the faint aroma of the tea. It would return in time, she thought. I will be able to smell the tea again. To eat properly once more. I will build myself up.

She ran her finger around the gold rim of the cup and sipped the tea thoughtfully. She glanced at the outside of the envelope.

Ranford?

Ranford School?

It meant nothing to her. Nonetheless, she picked up her paperknife to open the envelope. Like all her possessions, the paperknife was a quality instrument—neat leather handle, a perfectly functional blade designed to open envelopes cleanly, without being dangerously sharp.

She slid out a single sheet of thick, expensive paper. Addressed to her.

Dear Miss Kingswell,

This is to let you know that Ranford School is closing to all children and staff due to the virus epidemic.

What had that to do with her?

She crumpled the page, pushed it aside, and nibbled at the toast. She needed to do some shopping—and some more thinking.

She looked at her face in the mirror as she combed her hair off her face and sprayed it lightly so it would stay put. She had a good bone structure, she thought, and fine skin. She decided she would wear no more makeup—just a tinge of pinky-brown on her lips—and dress simply.

She found lightweight woollen checked trousers, a cream linen blouse, and a soft wool eggshell-blue sweater. Slipping her feet into strollers, she was ready to go. Her jacket—a dark brown leather—hung ready on the peg by the door.

She opened the drawer where they kept the money. Rolls of notes. Enough for now.

Then a small needle of doubt crept into her mind. What did anyone do for money if one was on one's own? In the corner of her spotless flat, the tools of her artist's trade were neatly stacked, but they did not provide her with a great living.

She dismissed further thoughts on that—for now.

Before she left, she made the breakfast area shipshape, rinsing the cup and plate and placing them on the draining board. She picked up the crumpled letter, which was clearly not meant for her, and smoothed it out.

Sebastian will be sent home for the duration until it is safe for schools to re-open.

Sebastian?

Who was Sebastian? Did she know a Sebastian?

Her mind, which only a short time ago had been clear, was no longer working so well. She read on.

He will be receiving work to do online and he will know how to access this.

She sought the date at the top of the letter. And the date today? The letter may have lain on the mat for a while. She had no idea. Was it possible that she was being held responsible for this—this—

Sebastian? Had someone rung the doorbell in vain and gone away? She dismissed the thought.

She tried to remember what age any Sebastian might be. There was no clue in the letter. She had a ridiculous image of a toddler, unable to reach up to the door knocker. No, he must be taller than that.

She needed to contact somebody. But who?

She went through the possibilities, proud in a silly way that she was still able to reason and function, at least a little. What were the options?

His father. Of course.

Then some suppressed information came flooding back to her. Some catty woman had recently said—what had she said now? *'I see your ex is in the papers.'* She had refused to read about it. But she was dimly aware that he had been in trouble—and perhaps gone to prison.

She had dismissed it from her mind. What was it to do with her? She had not seen him again since—how long ago? She had been a girl, a young girl, scarcely a woman. And he—what had he been? Not much more. And it was years ago. How many years ago?

She had made it clear that she wasn't going to be lumbered with a child. *He* could do what he liked with it. A faint memory returned. Had he asked his parents to care for it? Perhaps. Well, in that case, why hadn't the school written to them?

The thought returned. Elderly parents—perhaps they were dead. And the father—in prison?

She tried to dismiss any thought of responsibility.

Later on, she would phone the school. Just in case.

They were charming at the school. She spoke to the Headmaster's wife, a Mrs Clarke. She hadn't needed to explain anything. They said Sebastian was such a resourceful boy, but they did need to know where he was.

School could see that, wherever he actually was, he was accessing his study work online—she was able to see that—so he clearly was quite alright. She was not to worry.

It was possible that he had joined the family of a friend from school, but, if so, it was surprising that they had not been in touch with the school. She spoke the word *School* as though it were capitalised, as though it were the centre of the world.

She said again: she was not to worry. *Let School do the worrying.*

Not to worry. She had not worried—not for how many years was it?

She hadn't liked to ask how old this Sebastian was. They rang off, reassuring each other that either would let the other know if Sebastian made contact.

Would I know him if he made contact? she asked herself. *Would I know him?*

Chapter 7

Letters and Recollections

Living with a young grandson had brought a new and lively dimension to Mr Kingswell's everyday life. He felt the zip of life, the zest of excitement, the unpredictability of events, the anticipation of something new happening—all the time. He felt years younger. Even the daily post tumbling onto the mat with a thud caused a frisson of expectation.

Usually, as we ate breakfast, we heard the rattle of the letterbox and the thud as the letters fell onto the doormat. Grandfather went to pick up the post and carried the mail back to the kitchen, where we were still at the breakfast table, and inspected the day's haul. They were invariably for him. He got a lot of post. It was connected with his writing. He sifted through the pile of large brown foolscap envelopes and put them to one side to look at later.

His face lit up, seeing something unusual among the letters. He was in great good humour. Finding two small, ordinary white envelopes amongst the brown foolscap intrigued him.

'Here's two interesting ones, Spike!' he said, as he separated the two small white envelopes from the rest. 'Here's one. A slender envelope addressed simply to J. Kingswell. No title. Written in a bold, slanting, artistic script—possibly with a black draughtsman-style pen. A woman writing to me, I think, and not in any handwriting I recognise. I'm a bit of an amateur graphologist.'

He put it beside his plate.

'And—here's another one. Small white envelope, with the address written in strong, large cursive handwriting, turquoise ink, probably written with a fountain pen. And here's the clue—a Scottish stamp. I think it must be for you, Spike. Yes, it's an S, not a J. Look—S. Kingswell. No 'Mr' before the initial. I suppose 'Master' has become obsolete, like 'Esq.' for Esquire. It's definitely for you, Spike.'

He handed it over to me. 'One for you, I think.'

I received the letter with a small smile. It was lovely to get post. I looked at the Scottish stamp. I stuck my thumb under the flap of the envelope and, rather untidily, tore it open and read the letter to myself at the breakfast table—two sides written on one sheet of large folded A4 lined paper.

'Everything alright?' Grandfather asked.

'Of course,' I said, as I stuffed the letter back into the envelope to read again later and put it on my work table. 'It's from my

Housemaster. I get a hint that he's having a hard time living with his sister.'

Meanwhile, Grandfather was opening his own small white envelope neatly using a knife from the table. He drew out the single sheet of paper and read the few words on it to himself. He frowned.

'Oh dear! I should not have been surprised, Spike,' he said. 'Now I see who it is from. It's entirely my own fault. Delaying making contact with your school, then finding that they had sent information about the school's closure to my daughter. It's from…' He paused to emphasise the words. 'From Miss Alicia Kingswell. My daughter. Your mother, Spike. I haven't heard from her in fourteen or fifteen years.'

He read the few words she had written. Then he read them again—and again—trying to judge the thoughts that might have lain behind them. I could see he was distressed about what he had read. Or what lay behind it all.

'Well—she certainly has not addressed me as 'Dear Father'… but rather has gone straight into what she has to say. All said in just a few lines. It seems she proposes to call on us.'

At last, he read it out: *'I think in the light of all that is happening I shall need to come and see you. Alicia.'*

We were just finishing breakfast together, and Grandfather suggested we might take a fresh cup of tea into the study and sit and have a talk.

'You remember, soon after you first joined me, Spike, I said that I would tell you more about my daughter. Your mother…'

I held up my hands to try and stop him. 'Grandfather, I am not interested in hearing you talk about your daughter. It is no concern of mine. I really have no wish to hear anything.'

Grandfather was nonplussed. 'But I did say I would tell you about her when you first came.'

I looked at him as coldly as I could. 'Grandfather, when did you say you last saw her?'

'That is what I wanted to talk to you about. It is about fifteen years or so.'

'Grandfather, she is nothing to me,' I heard myself give a cold laugh. 'I have absolutely no curiosity about her at all. Quite the reverse. I want to hear nothing at all about her.' I paused, and then went on, 'And if you have not seen her for fifteen years, there is no need for you to have any curiosity about her either. So, why do we need to bring it up now?'

Grandfather probably realised that he could have exercised more tact in bringing the subject up. He sounded conciliatory.

'You know why, Spike. The school wrote to her to tell her they had to close because of the virus. They wrote to her because they know that your father is not in a position to give you a home. Not at the moment, anyway. He will want to as soon as he is able.'

I looked at Grandfather with new eyes. It meant a lot to me that Grandfather thought that my father would want to be available for me in the future.

'Do you think he will want to in the future, Grandfather?'

Grandfather seemed taken aback by my question. 'I am sure he will,' he said firmly.

'Good,' I said.

'There's no hurry,' said Grandfather. 'We have to wait for school to reopen, for now—and in the future, for your father to finish his prison sentence. In the meantime, we're alright here, I think.'

'Talking of my father and his situation makes me feel unsettled,' I said stiffly. 'Talking of my father upsets me. I have no idea really what he thinks. I can't bear it. And I really can't cope with you talking about… about other things.'

We both went quiet for a bit.

He read it out again—the contents of the letter: *'I think in the light of all that is happening I shall need to come and see you. Alicia.'*

'Spike, I am going to go and sit in my chair and cast my mind back to the time when my daughter departed from this house and examine my conscience. You are right. I'll do it alone. You carry on and get connected up with your online work from school.'

Chapter 8

Mr Kingswell Reflects.

Mr Kingswell said he was going to cast his mind back to the time when his daughter had departed from the house. As a seasoned academic, he drew out a sheet of A4 paper and began to set out the facts. After a time, he got lost in reminiscences—remembrances and regrets.

Looking back into the distant past, and seeing the events with fresh eyes now, he could see the irony: he, an acknowledged expert in the academic world, analysing in countless erudite writings the extraordinarily beneficial effects of access to education for children and its influence on society as a whole—whilst on the other hand, in his own family, events had played out before his very eyes. There was a yawning chasm between his work—the didactic opinions he expressed in specialist journals, conference lectures, and published books—and the way in which he had allowed his own family to experience such troublesome times. In truth, their life had unravelled into chaos. It was ever thus, he thought. Theory and practice—two different things.

But what were his plans now? How should he respond? What should be his strategy?

His grandson, Spike, was right. He should not inflict the burden of his past on others.

He thought logically. He needed first to go over his memories and recollect all that he could remember of the past, then get it straight in his mind.

Being an academic trained in historical analysis, he did what he would do to deconstruct any problem: he pulled out a pad of A4 paper and, with a pencil, began to jot notes and analyse the facts. He revisited the time—fifteen years ago—when he was summoned to his daughter's school to see, first, her form teacher, and then the Headmistress. Year 2005.

He had put it right out of his mind, consigned it to the back of his thoughts—something he never wanted to consider again. Even as he did so, the thought struck him that there was a terrible lack of humanity in the way he was analysing it now and, worse than that— far worse—was the cold, dispassionate way he had dealt with it then.

Going back to 2005: it was a dysfunctional household, but one he scarcely acknowledged as such.

Alicia had said to him,

'Miss Porter wants to speak to you, Father. My form-mistress. She said that you are to come and see her after school on a Friday. In fact, this Friday.'

'All right,' he had said, without looking up. 'Any idea what it's about?'

She looked at him. 'What do you think?'

'Not done your homework? Disruptive in lessons?'

'Don't be silly,' she had replied.

He had gone along, idiotically unprepared for what he was about to hear—an innocent entering the lion's den. Miss Porter sat at her teacher's desk in the empty classroom, and he was obliged to perch on one of the girls' desks in the front row.

'Have you any idea why I have asked you to come and see me?' she said softly, sounding almost sympathetic.

He shook his head. 'No.'

'Let me ask you first of all, if I may—how long is it since your wife left the household? Do you know where she is? And how do you think you are managing?'

He was tempted to ask what business it was of hers, but her inquiry had been so gently expressed that he felt it deserved a civil response.

'It's about five years,' he said. 'Alicia was ten. Maybe six years ago, then. She just walked out. I have no idea where she is. She did communicate to ask for access to money and funds, which was granted—later on via a solicitor—but otherwise no contact.'

When Miss Porter seemed to be waiting for a further response, he added, 'We're managing all right.'

'I don't think so,' Miss Porter had said firmly.

He was silent. Once again, he was tempted to ask what business it was of hers, but again was restrained by her gentle, sympathetic mien. As neither of them seemed to be going to enlarge on the situation, after a while, she spoke further.

'As teachers, we spot a child without a mother quite readily. She is the girl who comes to school with hair that has not been brushed, in a school blouse not well ironed, socks not pristine white, untidy, coming into morning school without having had her breakfast—and maybe not having a regular evening meal either—not bringing in any response to the notes from school that are sent home from time to time with the girls, sometimes hanging about with boys from the grammar school. Does that strike any chord with you?'

'I am sorry you feel like that,' he said. 'We have a daily who comes in once or twice a week. But I will certainly ask Alicia to be sure to hand me any notes from the school in the future.' He didn't like to say, *And I will tell her to brush her hair. And make herself some cereal in the morning.* For heaven's sake, how hard could it be to pour milk on cornflakes in a bowl?

'What is the name of your daily help?' Miss Porter asked more sweetly.

He recollected at once that the daily had given in her notice a few months ago, and nor could he remember her name. He had travelled abroad to attend a conference, he explained, and had not got round to replacing her since.

She asked, rather pointedly, if Alicia was doing the work of the daily since the last one had gone. She then asked if he thought Alicia had a boyfriend—and had Alicia perhaps had him to stay while she was left alone when he was at the conference.

He stared at her.

'What are you trying to say, Miss Porter?' he asked.

She looked at him very directly.

'Alicia has asked me to be the person to tell you that she is pregnant.'

There was, naturally, an appalled silence. He had no idea what to say. They sat without speaking for some time—uncomfortable— as he stared into the space before him, aware that her eyes never left his face. Minutes passed slowly.

Eventually, Miss Porter spoke.

'This is not, of course, the first time we have met this problem with one of our girls. In a moment or two, the Head Teacher would like to see you. But before I take you to her, and in the absence of any word from you, I would like to tell you what my response to the news was. I said to Alicia, 'How very sorry I was.' That could have been your words, Mr Kingswell.

'Alicia was one of our best pupils. She has a good brain. I like to think she would have gone on from this school to university and a future. Unfortunately, that is unlikely to be possible for her now.'

And then, when he still had no words to say, she added, 'Let me take you to the Headmistress now. There are some formalities to be discussed.'

The Headmistress had been firm, cold, and decisive. Alicia was to leave the school forthwith. It was not helpful for the other girls to have her in the classroom, amid gossip and talk about matters best left undiscussed.

'We have a school nurse, and Alicia has had an opportunity to talk to her about her options. She is an intelligent girl and knows what she wants—and indeed what she does not want. I am sure this has come as a shock to you, and it may be helpful if I tell you her decisions.

'She does not want a termination of her pregnancy, but neither does she want to be encumbered in the future with a child. So she has decided to go ahead with the pregnancy and delivery. The school nurse has been helpful and arranged for her accommodation. There are charities willing to assist.'

'Don't I have any say in this, Headmistress?'

'I don't think you do,' she said. 'I think you'll find when you get home that she has packed her things and gone.'

She didn't add *like your wife*, but she may have thought it.

'When this is all over, she may come back to you and ask your assistance in helping her towards applying for university entrance— and I imagine, with your academic background, you would be able to help. However, she will not be applying from this school.'

Mr Kingswell made no protest. Clearly, his daughter was being sent down from school in disgrace. Expelled.

'There is one further thing you should know. Though your daughter wants no further responsibility for a child in the future, I gather the boy who is involved has expressed a willingness to take an interest in the child—though, to be cynical, I don't imagine he will have the wherewithal.'

It was as the Headmistress had said. When he got back to his house, she had gone. Ascending the stairs to his daughter's room, he found she had taken all her things, and those items she could not carry away she had packed in a cardboard box and sealed with Sellotape. Later, he got a workman to stow the box up into the loft.

She had never contacted him for his help to get to university, and he had little knowledge of her life since. Like his wife, she had disappeared.

He had got his head down and continued to expand his delvings into his own academic field.

Chapter 9

Spike Has a Request

Though I had made it clear to my grandfather that I had no interest in talking about his daughter, who had written him a note, I did have another subject I wanted to speak to him about. I was eager to divert the talk onto something else.

'Let's take the tea into the study, Grandfather, and have a talk. It was a good idea. I do have something else I want to ask you.'

We settled in the study with a fresh pot of tea and cups and saucers on a tray. Once I had carried the tray in and set it down, I went back and brought two slices of Mrs Robinson's fruit cake on two plates. My grandfather poured the tea. He was happy to indulge me with a general talk.

'This is what I want to talk to you about, Grandfather. I want to visit my father in prison, and I can't go alone without an adult. It is not allowed. But if you write asking for a visit, you can ask to take me with you.' I fixed my eyes firmly on him. 'Please, Grandfather.'

'Why not?' said Grandfather at once. 'I've never been inside a prison, and I'm sure your father is a delightful man. As he is your father, he must be… well, I don't know what to say. I can't say he is a good man—or he wouldn't be in prison. But I'm sure he is a very interesting person, and I need to get to know him because he is your father.' Then he added, 'And we are getting on well together, I think, Spike, aren't we?'

I didn't feel I needed to respond to that.

Grandfather said, 'I will write the prison. But Spike, I hope you will help me out with this problem of my daughter. Looking back, I realise now that I didn't act very well towards her when she was young and in trouble. We all make mistakes, Spike. Your father has made a mistake that has landed him in prison, and I am sure he regrets it, because he is not free to take care of you when you need him, and doubtless for all sorts of other reasons. It is a terrible thing to lose one's freedom. And I was not thoughtful and kind to my daughter when she was young. It is too late to put that right. But because your school has written to her, I have to see her.'

'Grandfather, of course see her if you think you must. But I want nothing to do with it. I have to let you know that I have zero curiosity in that. I have no interest in seeing her. I just do not want to be involved. But if she is going to come here to see you, I can go to Mrs Robinson's in the Tower Block for tea. She has invited me to visit…'

I put on a voice like Mrs Robinson's and said, 'You must come and have tea with me one day,' she said, 'and see where I live.''

Grandfather smiled. 'You are honoured,' he said. 'She has never asked me.'

'She is on the 27th floor, and there is only one lift, and if it doesn't work, she has to walk up all those stairs. Or walk down—which is just as bad. And she should have an amazing view over London.'

It was settled then. Grandfather would see his daughter alone. And he would write to the prison requesting a visit for him and his grandson, which he did right away. He left it to me to make my own arrangements with Mrs Robinson.

I found Mrs Robinson easy to talk to. I propped myself up in the kitchen while she was working there.

'I've got two things to tell you and ask you,' I said. 'First, I have asked Grandfather to write and get permission for him and me to visit my father in prison.'

She didn't turn a hair. 'And what did he say?' she asked.

'He said he would,' I told her.

'I think that's an excellent idea,' she said.

I was pleased that she approved of the visit, thinking that she was clearly a woman of great experience of life.

'And the second thing?' she said.

'Could I come and have tea with you on Friday at three o'clock? His daughter is paying him a visit at three, and I don't want to be there.'

'Three o'clock is a bit early for tea,' she said. 'Come at three-thirty, and I'll give you a High Tea like they have up north. Walk over to the Estate—Baer Block. Take the lift. Twenty-seventh floor. Walk along the connecting corridor till you reach my door and ring the bell.'

It was all arranged.

Grandfather asked one more thing of me.

'Alicia is planning to be here Friday after lunch. About three. I don't know what we'll have to say to each other. But I wonder if you would go up the ladder to the loft space and get me down the box of her things. It's a cardboard carton, all Sellotaped up. Maybe dust the cobwebs off—it's been there fifteen years—or ask Mrs Robinson to see that it's clean. Alicia may want to look inside, or she may not. I think leave it on the floor at the back of the study or at the back of the hall. I'm not sure how big it is. I don't feel able to climb the loft ladder myself and carry it down.' He paused. 'I'll never forget you carrying down the little table from the top of the stairs when you first came. I couldn't even have lifted it.'

'No problem,' I said. And, as was always my way, I did it right away.

I found it quite interesting getting down the loft ladder, which folded down and was hinged from a ceiling flap in a clever way. Then, climbing up the rungs into the loft space, I found myself under the tiles of the roof and had a look around. I manhandled the bulky box down and stuck it at the back of the hall.

Grandfather said, 'I think I'll write and mention to her that you won't be here, but you'll be having tea with our housekeeper on the 27th floor of the local high-rise block. That way she won't be expecting to meet you.'

Grandfather mused aloud to me, 'It is possible, in fact, that Alicia feels exactly like you and that she is equally reluctant to come face to face—both of you privately feeling some relief that you would not be having to meet on Friday and decide what to say. More likely than not. On the other hand,' he went on, 'it may be that you both harbour a small germ of curiosity about the other, and of course, inadvertently, it is possible that your paths will cross one day and that you glimpse each other transiently. Who knows?'

Who knows? I thought. And said nothing.

Chapter 10

Alicia Visits.

Tea in The Tower Block

Alicia had come to Maida Vale by taxi. She was early. There was little traffic on the streets. She paid the driver over his shoulder with a note while sitting in the back of the cab, then opened the door to step out and go round to the window to get her change.

A few moments before, a boy had let himself out of the front door of her old home, walking down the short path and out of the gate, away along the pavement of Hamilton Terrace. She had already turned a little as she thanked the driver, paid him, and gave him a tip. They almost, but not quite, met.

Spike saw a slender young lady getting out of the taxi, a little taller than he was. Fair hair swung to her shoulders, swept back from her face; clean-cut features; a look of the English schoolgirl about her – fresh and not made-up – wearing a swing-back soft dark brown leather coat, a coloured silk scarf tucked in at the neck, sombre check trousers over brown polished casual shoes. No bag.

Alicia saw a handsome boy in his mid-teens, exuberant curly hair, and his face—she only had a transient glance—but, thinking about it later, she decided there was a little of her father when young, a little of the boyfriend of long ago whose love and friendship had derailed her and changed the course of her life. She saw, briefly, a soft vulnerability. She glimpsed some determination in him as he walked a few steps away up the pavement and stopped by the low brick wall.

She paused a moment as the taxi drove off, then turned and walked up the garden path to her childhood home, looking up at the pale green leaves and lilac-coloured flowers of the wisteria clambering over the porch. She tapped the knocker on the door—their old signal of three dots and a dash, the victory sign in Morse code—and within moments her father was at the door, holding it open. He stood back to let her in and, inadvertently, she said, 'Dad,' and kissed his cheek. He looked older, and his cheeks were wet with tears.

'Look at you,' he said. 'How beautiful you are!'

'Nonsense, Dad,' she said, and having called him 'Dad', she couldn't stop.

'We've made a tray of tea,' he said, and made for the kitchen.

She followed him, watched the kettle boil, saw him warm the pot and rinse it out, spoon in the tea leaves and drench them with freshly boiled water.

'Three minutes,' he said.

'Let me carry the tray.'

They sat in the study. Waited, and poured the tea as each liked it—he with a dash of milk, she without. Neither with sugar. On two plates, incongruously, lay the slices of Mrs Robinson's fruit cake.

'Spike laid the tea tray,' he explained. 'The appetite of boys!'

'Spike?'

'Sebastian Peregrine Kingswell. Not his choice of names, as he explained to me when we met—but SPK, so his friends call him Spike. Who named him?'

'I'd forgotten. His father registered his birth. So I imagine it was he. Quite romantic,' she grimaced.

'Before we move on, I should say how sorry I am. I am sorry. I was running an inadequate, disorganised household after your mother left, and I didn't look after you properly.'

'Dad, we both did our best. It was a good school and I had a good education. I messed up.'

'You're still a young woman. You can still go back. What did you do after?'

'I went to Art College. It was something you could do without support from your school and without qualifications. Though I did, in fact, do my A-levels as an external candidate, heavily pregnant, and met with some of my school friends during the Practicals. That was an eye-opener. Some greeted me like the old friends we had been, some snootily turned away. And not always the ones you would think, either. I did alright too. I passed with an A and two Bs.'

Her father asked cautiously, 'Has that given you a living? Art College. Have you worked at that?'

'I have done some illustration work. There is not a lot of money in it—not what I would call a career. I have lived with some rich friends.' She thought on, but was not ready to share her life and concerns with her father. 'I live alone in a lovely flat. I am not entirely sure whether it is mine to possess solo or not. I hope so.'

'We got your cardboard box down from the loft, Alicia. We were not sure whether you would like to look inside, and whether there are things you would like to take—now—or later. It is all as you left it.'

'I'll have another cup of tea, if you'll pour it. That cake was rather filling. But very good. Yes, there were some things I wish I had taken. I could just look now and take one or two. I can have a proper look another time. I can't carry the rest away today.'

'You don't need to. I see Spike has put out a stout knife for you to open the box.'

'Spike,' she said. 'What is he like? This boy. This young man. He has not had a very auspicious start in life.'

'Through no help of yours. Nor of mine. And no criticisms intended—of you or of me. But he has done alright. It seems he had a very stable early upbringing with the very ordinary elderly parents of his father—with the father flitting in from time to time, adding romance.'

'I met them once, the elderly parents. Years ago. They felt it was the correct thing to do. But honestly, to bring a toddler to meet a strange young girl who was still a teenager and still mixed up... it was a disaster.'

Her father smiled. It was the word Spike had used. *A disaster.* He went on, 'Then I gather the old lady got ill and died, and the old man felt he could not cope with the boy on his own. But his father found him a place at this school, which seems to have been a second home for him.'

'I spoke to them on the phone, the school. I was impressed. They sounded like a very caring and responsible set-up.'

'I gather his father has paid all his school fees in advance. Somewhat of a relief.'

Alicia smiled. 'Quite so.' She spoke thoughtfully. 'You know, a minor English public school is a haven. When I say minor, I mean no disrespect. But he will have the advantage of the caring, home-like feeling of a smaller school, and the education is still second to none—as good as the best. Provided he gets into a good House.'

'He seems to have done that. He's had a letter from his Housemaster at the sister's place in the Highlands. He asked the Headmaster's wife, the indomitable Mrs Clarke, for the address and, quite properly, she seems to have provided it via the Housemaster himself—leaving it to him to give out the contact if he doesn't mind being troubled.'

'Mrs Clarke was very sweet to me. Kept telling me not to worry. To let the school do the worrying. I didn't like to say to her that I hadn't done any worrying for the last fourteen years. Quite possibly she knows that. But still, she was intent on reassuring me. So strange that I have been drawn into this after all this long time. She emphasised how resourceful he was—and I suppose he was, to have found you. For that matter, how did he come to you?'

'To tell you the truth, I'm not quite sure.' And as he reflected, he really wasn't sure. 'My Mrs Robinson, who 'does' for me, was very suspicious when he first turned up, all dusty from having slept out as a homeless for a night. She made him produce his identity. I gather he produced his school library card, which had his name on it. Well, I don't think there's any doubt that he is who he says he is!'

'I hadn't thought of that!'

'Now, let's get down to opening the box, if you want to see if there's anything you want to take now.'

Kneeling on the floor on hands and knees, she sifted through the contents of the box. She selected only a handful of things to take away but had to ask for a bag to put them in. They found a shopping bag of sorts from Mrs Robinson's collection in the kitchen. Amongst the things she took was a framed photograph of her own mother. She showed it to her father.

'In better days,' Alicia said. 'What became of her?' she asked. 'Do you know anything?'

'I don't,' said her father. 'No more than we knew then. But we can enquire via the solicitor when you feel ready and if you want to. For myself, I've respected her decision to live separately. She continues to draw money to live on. But no, I have no idea.'

'I'll go, Dad. I'll be on my way.' She got up off her knees. 'I'll be in touch again. No, I don't need a cab. I'll walk.' And off she went.

He carried the tea tray back to the kitchen and got the roll of Sellotape out of the desk drawer to seal again the box of the memories of her childhood—not using it, just leaving it lying on the carton in the back of the hall.

Meanwhile, the tea party was arranged.

Mrs Robinson said she was happy to have me come for tea on the Friday afternoon of Grandfather's daughter's visit.

'Three o'clock is a bit early for tea,' she had said. 'I suggest three-thirty.'

I had planned to leave Grandfather's house about three and stroll slowly over to the Estate at the end of the road. I needed to be gone from Grandfather's house before the time when the daughter was expected. Now I had just transiently seen her, I was able to deliberately put all thoughts of the visit of Grandfather's daughter out of my mind. I had been curious to catch a glimpse of her. Now I had just clapped eyes on her, I dismissed all further thoughts.

I walked purposefully up the tree-lined avenue in Maida Vale. The road was generously wide and the centre had been planted with plane trees that shed their sticky burrs over the ground. Occasional weeds sprouted in the dry earth around the roots of the trees. A slight breeze rustled their leaves. It is wonderful, I thought, to have trees lining a street. It makes it a pleasant road to live in.

At the end of the avenue, I turned and crossed over the main road and walked down an alleyway into the council estate. I had been there once before, part of the way to carry some shopping bags for Mrs Robinson.

It is to enter a different world, I thought. At once, three tower blocks rise before you—immense, featureless, menacing fortresses separated by empty spaces that hold nothing at all. If a giant dinosaur or a pterodactyl were to lumber out from between the buildings, it would not have surprised me. It is an apocalyptic scene. The ground below is of solid tarmac, in which no weed has dared to break through. Not a tree nor a bush is in sight.

Approaching the first of the blocks, I could see that the elevation, which at first had looked featureless, was in fact speckled with dots and stripes that reveal themselves—on looking up and squinting higher and higher—to be windows, like numbers of small, unseeing eyes embedded in the surface and joined together by strips linking crossways. These are the balconies and walkways between the flats.

I walked further around. It is not at first obvious to an outsider where the front of the building should be, but once located, the name of the block is there in surprisingly small letters: *Baer Block.* There seems to be no one about. No one strolls between the blocks or rides bicycles over the flat surface. There are no benches to sit on.

I entered the narrow entrance lobby and there was the lift: a single metal door. The stairs were alongside—red brick, going round and round the lift shaft, with a round handrail on one side made of cold iron. I pressed the button for the lift. It took a while to arrive, and there was no whirring sound to indicate whether it was on its way. But it was worth the wait when I considered the climb to the twenty-seventh floor.

It came at last with a judder, and I was relieved to find no one inside. I stepped in and pressed for floor 27. It shuddered into action. The lift smelt faintly of antiseptic—or possibly urine.

Once I stepped out of the lift at floor twenty-seven, I followed the walkway along the open corridor, passing other front doors until I found her number. One or two of the doors had been heavily reinforced with steel locks and barriers. I rang her doorbell. It gave a melodious musical chime, and then Mrs Robinson was opening her door and welcoming me in.

Her flat was not at all what I had expected.

Mrs Robinson knew how to give a warm welcome. She greeted me as a special guest and had tea laid out on a small oval folding table, covered with an embroidered tablecloth. The flat was warm and carpeted with a rosy, thick floral carpet. She had a comfortable sofa with lots of cushions, which she proudly explained could be opened up to make a bed.

'So if you are ever stuck with nowhere to stay again, there's always a bed for you here!' she said.

Although there was no fireplace as such—no grate—there was a hearth where the electric fire could stand, and a mantelpiece. On the wall above it she had three porcelain ducks in flight: different sizes from large to smaller, slanting upwards, looking as though they were flying off into the distance.

On the mantelshelf were china figures: a shepherdess with a lamb, a milkmaid with buckets, a small brown beagle dog, a Scottie, a rough white poodle that had to stand on a silver three penny bit to bring luck, three small green horses, and an ivory figure—all clearly treasures. In the centre was a clock. I admired them all and heard their histories.

We settled down to tea. Mrs Robinson said she had prepared a high tea, such as they have in the north—steaming hot kippers in butter with white bread and butter, large china cups of tea, bread and butter with damson jam. All excellent.

While we ate, she told me the story of her life. By the time we had finished, I felt I knew all about the Robinson family. Her parents were now deceased—'passed,' as she called it. She had been one of five, she told me. She talked non-stop about her brothers and sisters: their names, their characteristics, who they had married, their children. She herself had no children, but plenty of nieces and nephews, and she was full of entertaining stories about all of them.

I wondered about the late Mr Robinson, but apparently he was not part of the story.

'There are always secrets in any family,' Mrs Robinson declared.

There was such a bewildering number of her relatives, I said, 'I think I'll make a family tree for you, Mrs Robinson. That way we'll sort out who's who.' She was pleased with the idea when I explained how I would draw it out.

She paused for breath when she was ready to bring out a slice of her favoured cake. Silence fell.

'Then what about you, Spike?' she said. 'Your turn.'

'You know about me,' he said. 'I've got nobody.'

'That's not true,' she said. 'You've transformed your grandfather's life. He was getting to be an old recluse. And he's re-joined the human race since you came. And you didn't even know him before.'

'We do get on alright. I remember what you said to me when I had told you once that I was no trouble. You said I should be grateful to him for taking me in. And I am.

'Living in school, I had forgotten what it was like to have a home to live in. A home as well as the school. And to have a bedroom all of my own. It's a bed in a dormitory, of course, at school—with other boys. I had forgotten what it was like to have a room of my own.'

'And your father will come out, Spike. It's wonderful that you're going to go and see him. It will mean a great deal to him. It's a hard thing to be deprived of your liberty—particularly for someone like your father, who sounds as though he were a bit of a free spirit.'

'That is a good word for him, Mrs Robinson. A free spirit. I said to Grandfather, my father was like a spark of lightning. He would turn up at Pat and Tony's house, light up the whole house—we never knew when he was coming—then a few days of excitement, sometimes just a few hours.

'I had to go to school. And then he was off again. There's lots I will want to tell him if we get to go and see him.'

'Well, I'm looking forward to meeting your father one day!'

We had a piece of her cake, and she added hot water to her teapot, gave it a stir, and poured us another cup of tea each.

'You see, you've got more family than you think. That other grandfather who brought you up—when he's got over the shock and sadness of losing his wife—he'll be wanting to see you again. His grief will lessen, and he will want to see you. Just not to have the daily care of you. You owe him a lot, looking after you all those years. You must look him up—maybe not at this time, but later on, definitely, when everything has settled down.'

She showed me the rest of her flat: a bedroom with a pink candlewick bedspread, bathroom, and kitchen. At first, she declined my offer to help with clearing the tea things away and washing up, but then she said, 'Oh, go on. Take a tea towel and dry for me. We'll just get the plates and cups and saucers done.'

When we were finished, she asked, 'And what do you think of my flat?'

'It's just smashing,' I said. 'Right cool.' She was pleased with that.

Then she said, 'Do you want me to walk down with you? I'll see you off.'

'No, I'll make my own way. Thanks, Mrs Robinson. I don't think I've ever been invited to a tea like this before. Thank you so much.'

I made my way to the lift and out into the open again. As I walked through the empty spaces between the tower blocks, it was not quite so deserted now—there were a few people around, coming home from work, moving purposefully towards one or other of the towers.

I still found it a strange and alien place. I was glad to cross the main road and walk in the twilight down between the trees of my avenue and reach Grandfather's house. I ducked under the wisteria in the porch and was pleased to find Grandfather alone.

'Did you have a nice time?' he asked.

'I did,' I said. 'Like nothing I've ever experienced before.'

I didn't enlarge on that.

I offered to take the box back up the ladder to the loft, but Grandfather said she had only taken one or two things—a small framed photograph of her mother, who had walked out on them when Alicia was aged ten or thereabouts—and one or two other things. So, while it had been worthwhile getting it down, and it had been much appreciated, she might come back for more.

'Don't Sellotape it up again for the moment. We'll just leave it there at the back of the hall. It's not in anybody's way. She may come back and go through her things again and want to take something more out of it.'

The box was to stay where it was, at the back of the hall.

Chapter 11
The Prison Visit

The authorisation for the prison visit came swiftly. It surprised us both. We were given a date and a time.

'We should take him something. Any ideas what he would like?'

I looked blankly at my grandfather. 'Take him what?'

'I'm just thinking that in books I've read describing visits to a prison, relatives take cigarettes, I think, or chocolate, or books, or a mobile phone, or—other things. And maybe if they don't want them, they trade them with other inmates.'

Seeing my horrified expression, he added, 'Are you sure you want to go? It is prison, you know.'

'Yes, of course I want to go. I just hadn't thought about that.'

'Well, let's see. Does he smoke, Spike?'

To his horror, I almost began to cry.

'Look here, Spike. This is going to be too much for you. Let's put it off for a bit.'

I gathered myself. 'It's not that,' I said. 'It's just that I don't know if he smokes or not. You'd think I would know that about him. But I don't. He wouldn't smoke in front of me, anyway.'

'Well, maybe cigarettes aren't a good idea. We'll take some chocolate—dark chocolate or fruit and nut milk chocolate.'

I had gathered my composure and was ready to offer an explanation.

'The truth is, Grandfather, I don't know him very well in that way. I don't know his tastes. I wouldn't know if he likes dark chocolate or milky fruit and nut, or what books he likes to read, or if he reads magazines or comics, or smokes, or anything. When he came to see us at Pat and Tony's, it was always a fleeting visit. Usually, we didn't even know he was coming. He wasn't expected—he just appeared like a whirlwind and everything stopped and was busy. Pat fussed around him, and Tony and he talked. I still had to go to school, and when I came home, he was often gone.'

Grandfather nodded. 'Fair enough! Fair enough! When did you last see him, Spike?'

'A year or two ago, I think. Two, maybe even three. When he took me to see Ranford School. We met the Headmaster and Mrs Clarke and picked my House. I've just had a brilliant idea though. Mrs Clarke is a JP—that's a Judge, you know—and she'll certainly have visited prisons. She'll know what sort of things would be best to take.'

'Good thinking! She might even have a suggestion on his taste in literature, what books he might like to read. We've never really talked about him, you and I. Did your father go to university, do you know?'

'He did. No—I think he did. He is very clever. And lively, I should say. Very lively. And smiley.'

'Well, I look forward to meeting him.'

Mrs Clarke was indeed helpful. First of all, she said she would immediately make up a duplicate of Sebastian's student identification card, which included his photograph, and send it to us by post. We were to take that along, together with Mr Kingswell's own passport for identity. She said we would certainly not be allowed in without those, and the letter of authorisation.

She thought the permission had come through so quickly possibly because of the virus. However, she explained that we would not be allowed to take along any presents of the sort Grandfather was planning, or that he had read about in fiction.

She did, though, recommend taking some £1 coins for a locker to deposit our valuables in, and lots of loose change, as there would probably be a tea bar where we could buy cups of tea, coffee, or hot chocolate, and maybe a snack. She warned us they could be quite expensive for a little wrapped cake or biscuit. Expensive or not, it sounded quite cheerful.

The things Grandfather had read about—the two bars of soap, the couple of face flannels, the man's hairbrush (just a cheap one), the couple of combs, two blocks of chocolate, magazines and paperbacks of a spy thriller set abroad—she said were the sort of things a prisoner might like to organise for himself before he went in, maybe together with a notepad and pencils.

Nor did she think that prison was necessarily the ideal place to embark on serious reading. In fact, when Mr Kingswell thought further on it, he reflected that the recommended gifts he'd read about in fiction for an inmate might have been intended for someone imprisoned abroad, or incarcerated in a hospital or mental asylum under compulsory order—someone sectioned under the Mental Health Act—which was not the same sort of thing as a prisoner in a criminal case. Or maybe the taking of useful presents to a prisoner was harking back to the Victorian age or the long-ago times Grandfather researched in. They certainly weren't allowed now.

Mrs Clarke said to Grandfather that she had found it a good idea to think of topics of conversation they might both like to have before getting there. The visit was usually only one hour, and if you didn't make any plans beforehand, you could find yourself lost for things to talk about for the first half of the visit—and then rapidly come to the end and feel there was lots unsaid that you should have got round to.

'Well done, Spike, with your idea to phone Mrs Clarke. She's a fountain of knowledge.'

She was also a highly intelligent and thoughtful woman—knowledgeable and kind. When we opened the stiff white envelope containing Spike's student identification card, we found she had sent two versions: one with my name finishing with Kingswell, the other with my father's surname added also. She left it to us to decide which to use in different circumstances.

We took a taxi to the prison—Wormwood Scrubs. It wasn't far from Maida Vale. The taxi driver didn't turn a hair.

'The Scrubs? Visitors' Entrance?' he queried.

We agreed. He dropped us off with a 'Good luck!' and we felt cheered by the matter-of-fact way he had received the reason for our going there. It was certainly not the first time he had taken fares for a prison visit—all in a day's work for him.

The visit itself was an extraordinary experience—for both of us.

We went together into the Visitors' Centre and realised we were on the early side, perhaps half an hour early, but that seemed to be quite acceptable. We presented our letter and our identification papers to the woman at the reception desk. She was in full prison uniform and took them with a smile. She seemed a cheerful person and gave us each a form to fill in and sign.

We each produced a biro from our pockets—well prepared—and once signed, we were directed to the lockers where Grandfather deposited his wallet and house keys, keeping a trouser pocket full of loose change and a note or two in his jacket pocket. Then we sat together and waited until we were called.

There were other visitors coming and going—one woman with a whole family of small children who ran around—but mostly there was one person on their own: a mother perhaps visiting a son who had got into trouble, or a young woman visiting her husband or boyfriend.

Our names—mine and Grandfather's—were eventually called, and we both stood and had metal detectors passed over us, and then were patted down. Grandfather deposited his loose change and his locker key into a basket to go through a further check. He picked it up on the other side and put everything back into his jacket pocket. It was rather like an airport check at the boarding gate.

Two dog handlers brought their dogs over on a lead to sniff at us—one a retriever, one a large German Shepherd dog, an Alsatian—but neither seemed concerned with us. We had passed muster.

Then we were allowed through the push-button doors into the Visitors' Hall, and at last, we were there. Before us, on the other side of the room, sat the prisoners awaiting their guests in a long line. A row of men were seated on chairs, a wooden table before each, and a chair or two on the visitors' side. Mrs Clarke, the Headmaster's wife, had not prepared us for this situation.

For a terrible moment, Grandfather and I stood, rooted to the spot, wondering how we would know which of the men— and they were all men—sitting patiently on their chairs was ours. I realised that Grandfather had no idea what the man we were looking for looked like, and it had been a few years since I had last seen my father. I didn't know how prison might have changed him. The thought went through both our heads: Was this going to be like an identity parade in reverse, where we walk along the row until one of them recognises us? Or would we need to go to the prison officer sitting on a raised platform to one side, with his dog alongside, looking disinterested, and ask him to point out who it was we should be visiting?

I felt Grandfather falter at my side. Then, in a moment of inspiration, he said,

'The clue is in the chairs!'

The first desk on the left had a great cluster of chairs opposite, probably for the woman with all the children, and sure enough, they were making a beeline toward him. Her prisoner husband, on the other side of the table, looked like a rough, defeated sort of man. Along the whole row, most of the prisoners had a single chair opposite, waiting just for a mother, wife, or girlfriend.

Towards the centre, there was a prisoner who had two visitor chairs drawn up ready on the opposite side of the table. We were two visitors, and Grandfather, looking at the man, thought he looked like a possibility in age and appearance for the man we were looking for. He started out tentatively toward him. To our immense relief, we saw the man gazing with a huge grin on his face at me. We had got our man.

The prisoners weren't allowed to stand up, apparently, but he stretched out his hand in a sort of handshake. We were allowed a quick hug across the table.

'Dad!' I said. I could see now it was him. A bit different.

'It's good to see you,' said my father. 'I want to hear all the news.'

'I'll get us all some tea, and a wrapped cake and biscuits,' said Grandfather, starting to move toward the tea bar. 'Are you happy with tea, or do you want coffee or hot chocolate?'

'Hot chocolate would be nice, Grandfather,' I said, without taking my eyes off my father. Yes, I could see it was him.

'Tea would be fine, and I do want to thank you, Mr Kingswell, so much for bringing him.'

As Grandfather walked to and fro, collecting two cups of tea and a hot chocolate for me, along with an assortment of cellophane-wrapped cake and biscuits, we reflected that Mrs Clarke had been wrong about one thing. We hadn't needed to worry about practising topics of conversation and thinking of things to say.

We were talking non-stop.

Chapter 12

Secret Request

Grandfather and I came home to Maida Vale in a sombre and reflective mood after the prison visit to my father. When we had come out of the Visitors' Centre, we found a small rank of taxis outside. It seemed easier to take one than walk to the bus stop and wait around.

Mrs Robinson had a tray of tea things ready for our return, and I went into the kitchen with her to make the tea.

'How did you get on?' she asked me.

'It was alright,' I said. 'Mrs Robinson, have you ever done a prison visit?'

'Bless you, dear, I have. Many times. As have many others on my estate. And it doesn't get any easier with each time. Did you find your father in good spirits?'

'I should say so. He usually is in good spirits. If he has to serve four years, I'll be almost finished school by then.'

'It's likely he'll be out long before then.'

'Maybe. Or maybe not. It was good of him to settle my school fees before he went down. But he says he still has things to organise outside, and I could help. He asked me to do something for him.'

'Good gracious! What did your grandfather say about that?'

'He didn't hear. You know Grandfather—he was very courteous. He felt the visit was about Dad and me, and he busied himself getting us stuff from the tea bar and allowed us to have a private conversation. But if I collect something for Dad, I have to check that I'm not observed, look out that I'm not followed, maybe take someone with me, and hide it well away afterwards.'

'That doesn't sound a very safe thing for a boy to do. Are you going to tell your grandfather?'

'Not tonight anyway. It was good of him to come with me. I don't think they would have let me in without an adult along. Neither of us had ever done a prison visit before. As you've done one, you know all the business—the metal detectors, the patting down, the dogs—and when we got in, there was this row of men on chairs, each one before a small wooden table—well, you know, you've been there—and neither Grandfather nor I knew which was our man! It's more than two years since I last saw Dad, and of course Grandfather doesn't know him. I don't know how Grandfather knew, but he set out walking toward him and then I saw Dad grinning and holding out his hand to me.'

'The tea's ready. I'll carry it in. Then I'll leave you to it.' She paused. 'Where would you hide this thing you're to collect, anyway? How big is it?'

'I don't know. Up the loft ladder with Alicia's box? Or in your flat on the estate, with all your treasures on the mantel shelf?'

She laughed. 'And not for the first time! You take care!' Then, as we went into the study and she laid the tea tray down, she said, 'I think you should tell your grandfather all about it.'

'Tell me all about what?' said Grandfather.

But she was gone.

'She was just asking me about the visit,' I said.

Chapter 13

Room 4D

I had a mission to fulfil. For my father. I had only the vaguest information about what it was I had to do and how to go about it, but I was determined to carry it through if I could.

My father had dropped his voice a little as he muttered an address: 4D Marchmont House, Little Great Middleton Street, EC1, was what I thought he had said. He had asked me to retrieve a metal box secreted there in the rafters and warned me that the area where it was hidden was used by dangerous people who stored their own things there and guarded the building. He told me I should not tangle with them.

I sat on the edge of my bed and wrote as much of the address as I could remember on the notepad on my bedside table. I had a well-thumbed paperback, an A-Z of London, in my hands. I had found it in the kitchen alongside the cookery books. There had been nothing helpful among the volumes on the library bookshelves in the study, but I had discovered the A-Z propped up together with a Local Business Guide on the kitchen shelves. I looked first at the EC1 area on the maps and saw nothing that stood out to me. I turned to the Index at the back. It took some searching, down and down through the index, to find anything that remotely resembled the address my father had mentioned. Little Great Middleton Street, EC1, was what I thought he had said, leading to a small park.

So, I began the search for Little Great Middleton Street. There was no street in the index under Middleton that looked relevant, and Little Great did not yield anything either. But eventually, after practically reading through the whole index, I came across something that looked hopeful in the EC1 area. I turned down the corner of the page of the map where I had located an area where I thought it could possibly be. It was not easily identifiable on the map, as the street was so small. There seemed to be a tiny alleyway off Gray's Inn Road. My father had said it was a cobbled yard, a cul-de-sac, leading nowhere in particular, but at the end was a sort of small park with open spaces. And that looked like a possible match on the map, though the yard did not show any entry to the green space. However, it did seem to be there at the end. 'Good way to make your escape through that park once you have secured the trophy,' my father had said, with a smile and a sideways shake of his head.

I thought I would go first and see if I could even find the place and check if it was Little Great Middleton and if there was a Marchmont House there. Even if it were the right place, I needed to know more—see what the neighbourhood was like, whether there were people coming or going, habitually hanging about outside, and at what times of day people lived there. Whatever it was that had been deposited there might have been put there years ago. Maybe even by now, it was gone.

I had to fit my reconnaissance visits in with the online lessons from school. They were beamed out to all boys constantly and required our presence and response. They were my priority, for sure.

EC1 was a good distance away from Hamilton Terrace. We in Maida Vale were NW8. It took a good amount of time to get across London. A bicycle would have been a great asset, I couldn't help feeling. I thought I might ask Mrs Robinson about that.

Little Great Middleton Street, when I found it, was not really a street as such. It was a cobbled yard that lay behind the buildings that lined Gray's Inn Road. It would have been easy to miss it altogether if one were looking for a street. It was approached through what might once have been a horse-drawn carriage access to old stables. I only ventured through the old carriageway gap between the two halves of the building because I spotted the words 'Marchmont House' high up in the red brickwork of the old building.

Through the carriageway I went, and there was indeed a small sign reading Little Great Middleton Street, and the 'street,' such as it was, was indeed cobbled, as my father had said, with no pavements on either side. Eureka! I had found it.

There was no one about—no sign of life. As I walked along, I could see the backs of the buildings were numbered 1, 2, 3, and 4, and all seemed to be the backs of Marchmont House. Perhaps they had been the stable boys' rooms in the days of horse and carriage and servants. Number 4 was at the far end of the terrace, right at the end, and beyond it there was a space and some rubble before the yard finished with a low fence. Beyond that, I could see the green space of a small park. That was just as my father had described. As I stood there and looked around, I knew for sure I had found the right place.

There was no gate through the fence to the park, but I judged that if I put one hand on the top of the fence, I could vault over quite easily into the park grounds.

Number 4 was a narrow building, the last of the row, and seemed to have just the one room on each floor. The entrance to it was an open lobby, not closed by any door. I looked into that open lobby, where there was one door on the left. The number 4A was daubed on it in black paint. A narrow wooden staircase led upwards, open to the outside. Behind the wooden stairs at the back of the lobby was a square butler's sink with a single cold tap and a toilet with a pull-chain to flush, ending with a white porcelain handle. The toilet had one of those half-doors, open at the top and the bottom, where you could see the feet and the heads of people using it.

Well, I was here. I might as well explore further. Quietly, I went up the narrow wooden stairs and found, on the first floor, a single door with the number 4B. Then, on the second floor, the same again—a single door, 4C, and finally, on the top floor, 4D, my target room, all numbered on the wood of each door in black paint. On that top floor, also, where the stairs finished, there was an open door to a sort of small cupboard—a cubbyhole more than a room—that housed a broom and a pan-and-brush, which presumably could be used to sweep the stairs and entrance clean. On the wall of the cubbyhole, hanging on a large hook, I saw a key.

I did not feel ready yet to investigate further on my own.

What would I have to do to progress to the next stage? I was hardly ready to think about that as yet. What were my options? Knock on the door of 4D? Use the key that hung in the cubbyhole? Enter and search with my hand into the space in the rafters above the door? For this, I felt I could do with some backup; someone with me, I thought.

Getting down to the area from home, there and back, was tiresome. I didn't have a lot of time after online school. I felt I needed two things: one—someone with me, and two—an easier way of getting there and back. I thought I would talk to Mrs Robinson about that and maybe also write to my Housemaster.

The deserted cobbled street, the back of the dingy tenement buildings, and the unpopulated area combined to convey a forbidding atmosphere. Frankly, I could not imagine for one moment my father walking over the cobbles of Little Great Middleton Street to deposit his treasure, whatever it was, at the top of the last building in the row. Perhaps he had got someone else to do it for him. One of his friends. I wished now I had asked him. But now my father was getting me to retrieve it.

I felt I had made some sort of a start by locating it, and I took myself straight back to Grandfather and Maida Vale and my online streaming schoolwork. I would think further about it later and come again another time.

Chapter 14

4A, 4B, 4C, 4D and the Heavies

I visited again the following week, and I sensed once more the forbidding atmosphere in Little Great Middleton Street. Between the cobbles, small weeds sprouted. There was no one about.

I resolved to check out the small green space at the far end and took myself easily over the fence into the park. I found a pleasant little park, an oasis of greenery with some small formal rose beds and other beds planted out with perennials, pansies, and stocks, by the Council. I wandered around it. There were benches to sit on and a small sandwich bar that did toasties of cheese and ham, meat pies, a soup-of-the-day that a blackboard announced as leek 'n' potato, filled baguettes, and other snacks. There were also, usefully, public toilets. I could imagine the local office workers coming at lunchtime on sunny days to sit and eat their sandwiches and drink their coffee. Here, there were even a few people about. One or two mothers were making a circuit around the grass lawns, strolling along the gravel paths, pushing their babies in pushchairs. An elderly man had laid claim to one of the benches and was reading his newspaper. The entrance, and for me most importantly, the exit of the park, was higher up the hill of Gray's Inn Road, nearer toward King's Cross. The pleasant nature of this little park, adjacent to the cobbled street, gave me a little reassurance—a contrast to the derelict and neglected tenements at the back of Marchmont Buildings in the cobbled cul-de-sac of Little Great Middleton Street.

I thought again of my father's request to retrieve the item for him, and I was determined to explore further and try to get it done.

Mrs Robinson, as anticipated, had good ideas when I asked her about the possibility of having the use of a bicycle.

I told her that I had located the place where I was meant to retrieve some object for my father and that it was a good distance away, and I could only get there once I had finished my online school.

She responded positively at once.

'One of my nephews,' she said, 'is not in a position to use his bike at the moment, and there is no reason, Spike, why you should not have the loan of it.'

She wheeled it round to Maida Vale.

'Why doesn't he need it for the moment?' I asked.

'Young offenders!' she said. 'He's in Feltham. Not for long. Just a short sharp shock,' and she smiled. 'Now he's the sort of chap you want to have with you when you're doing your recce to retrieve whatever it is for your dad. No flies on Darren.'

I gazed at her with awe. 'Do you think he'd be up for it when he comes out? I'd really appreciate having someone with me.'

'I'm sure he would. Darren is up for anything. And not always the right thing. That's why he's in Feltham. I'm not sure he's coming out yet a while though. Meanwhile, you take the bike and ride around and see how the land lies there.'

'Thanks ever so much, Mrs Robinson. Please let me know when Darren gets out, and I will certainly take him with me. That would make such a difference. I will also write my Housemaster about it. He's a really good bloke, and I'll ask him if he finds himself in London, if he would give me a hand, and watch my back. But I don't suppose he will be coming down to London. He's staying with his sister in the Highlands of Scotland, and I gather from his letter that she's finding it a bit of a strain. She's used to living on her own, and she didn't reckon on having her brother stay long-term.'

'There's a lot to be said for standing on your own two feet,' she said. 'How do you think your grandfather is coping, having you here all the time?'

She looked at her in astonishment. 'I'm no trouble, am I?' I said.

'Think on!' said Mrs Robinson. 'It's really good of him to have taken you in and given you a home. Make no mistake about it. You be grateful for it!'

That gave me something to think about.

Having the bike was a boon, and it meant I could cycle all over bits of London as well.

When I brought it back to Maida Vale, I realised that it might get stolen if I left it outside, even if chained up, so I wheeled it into the hall each time and propped it at the back by Alicia's box. It left a trail of wet bicycle tyre marks across from the front door to the back of the hall every time I came in, and it brought fluttering leaves and some mud with it.

Grandfather was very tolerant about it, and I remembered to thank him, reminded by Mrs Robinson's words that it was good of him to have taken me in.

With the bike, it was much easier and quicker to get down there and back, so I was able to get there earlier in the day.

At my next visit, I entered the lobby again, and before I had time to hesitate, I bounded up the stairs. The doors on each level were closed. I presumed they were locked. This time, though, there was no key hanging in the cubbyhole, and I thought I could hear that someone was in Room 4D. And it was into that room, 4D, that I knew I had been asked to go. I needed to ensure first that when I went in, it was unoccupied. I went over in my mind what I needed to do to retrieve that trophy—my father's small tin box—that he had said was tucked above the door lintel, I thought he had said, on the sloping roof under the rafters.

I had been up and down the stairs a few times now. Sometimes the key was hanging there. Often, though, it was not. No key there. It dawned on me that when the key was not there, I could often hear someone moving around inside Room 4D. If the occupant went out, then he locked the door and hung the key in the cubbyhole. And so, I reasoned, it was likely, possible at least, that if the key was there, the occupant had gone out and I would have a short time to unlock the door and retrieve the object.

Still, I was not quite ready to risk that action.

As I came down the stairs, the door to Room A on the ground floor opened, and the inhabitant peered out. It was the first time I had seen anyone about. She was a little old lady, shrunken and small, no taller than myself—tiny and bent, with a markedly curved back and her head held rigidly forward on her neck and spine. She was so bent that, in order to meet my eye, she had to tilt her face up because her head was unable to move on its pivot. Wispy white hair grew sparsely on her scalp. For all her frailty, though, her eyes met mine with a lively, inquisitive glance.

'You looking for someone?' she asked. 'Or are you looking for somewhere to stay?'

I followed her lead. 'Is there a room free?'

'The chap in the top will be down shortly—that's Alf. He hands out the evening newspaper at the tube station for a few hours. Mr Tough Guy in Room C is around and about. Maybe Room B will be moving on. Or has gone already. You never know. You're welcome to sit in my armchair for a while if you want to take the weight off your feet. I'm always looking for someone to talk with. I get lonely.'

She invited me in with a nod of her head. It was just the one room, with a bed on the far side. I sat in the decrepit old armchair. We left the door open, waiting for Alf to come down.

'I'm Annie,' she said. We sat and talked.

Generally, I felt I was not good at conversation; I thought I had no small talk, but my time having tea with Mrs Robinson had paid dividends.

'Tell me about your family,' I said. 'Where are they living now?' She launched into a lengthy recount, and once again I had a plethora of names—children and grandchildren, their names, relationships, and exploits—until I had to say, as I had done to Mrs Robinson, 'I should need to make a family tree for you in order for me to get them all straight.' She knew at once what I meant —a bright little lady— and invited me to do so.

'Here comes our friend,' she said. 'Off to work.' And through the open door, the gaunt figure of the newspaper seller could be seen coming down the stairs.

The newspaper man looked in on the old lady as he passed. 'I'm off now, Annie. See you later,' he said. 'Got a visitor, have you?'

'I have,' she said. 'We've had a good talk. He's going to make me a family tree. That's Alf,' she explained.

'It's been nice to talk with you,' I said. 'I'll just go up to the top of the stairs for a moment.'

I wanted to check my explanation on the presence or absence of the key. As Alf had just gone out, if my theory about the key was correct, it should be there now, hanging on the hook. When I had gone up there before and Alf was in his room, the key had not been there. Now that he had just left, if I was right, the key would be back on the hook. And indeed it was. The key was there, hanging on the hook in the cubicle.

I had clattered up to the top floor, but before I could even think of unhooking it, the door of Room C opened, and a thick-set, broad man in a singlet and trousers came out and stood on the stairs, blocking my way down with his massive size.

'What are you doing here, sunshine?' he boomed in a far from friendly manner.

'I've just been talking to the little lady in Room A,' I said.

'We've been 'aving a talk,' she called up. 'He might look into Room B if he moves on. It's nice for me to 'ave someone to talk to.'

'What do you want in the broom cupboard?'

'Just looking.'

''Just looking' can take a broom and sweep down the landing and stairs, then,' he said.

I gave a short laugh. 'Why not?' I said.

I seized the broom and did just that—swept the top landing and down the stairs—then used the pan and brush at the bottom and emptied the pan into the rubble at the side of the building. As I knocked the dust out of the pan, I heard a tinkle of noise and saw a glimmer of something shiny that caught my eye, shimmering among the twigs and rubbish. I bent to pick it up—a tiny key—and put it in my pocket.

The little old lady was hovering at her doorway. 'The heavies have come back,' she said. And sure enough, two hefty-looking blokes were propping themselves up opposite the end of tenement number 4, a can of Red Bull in one hand, caps on each head worn backwards.

Why are they here?'

'Looking after their territory,' she said. 'They come and they go. Eric's gone back in,' she said.

Eric was clearly the big fellow from Room C. It was clearly not the time to try to take the key from the broom cupboard and enter Room D to look for the hidden tin box with the heavies stationed outside.

I was not sure when would be best. Ideally, I thought, I would like to do it with a look-out chum who could watch my back, but I had no one suitable.

Once more, I took myself back to Hamilton Terrace.

Chapter

15 Back-Ups

Grandfather was immersed in his writing and clearly didn't want to be disturbed. I finished off my schoolwork online and then, sitting there, I decided to write to my Housemaster, up in the Highlands of Scotland, where he was staying in his family house with his sister. I had lots to tell him.

I would write first about how well suited I was to living with my grandfather. Then I would sound him out to see whether he might be coming down to London and be available as a back-up.

Dear Mr Benson,

Thank you for your letter. I am glad you have settled in with your sister. I am sure she is really very pleased to have you living there. It is not always easy learning to live with someone else when you have enjoyed being on your own. But hopefully, it will not be forever.

This is to let you know where I have landed up since school closed down. You probably don't remember, but you said to me once that we all have two grandfathers and I should look up in the library the grandfather who had the same surname as mine—well, one of my names—and I was so grateful to you for telling me that and for reading about him.

Along with an account of his work, I found his address. I put a letter of introduction through his letterbox and, having been vetted by the lady who does for him—Mrs Robinson—she's a bit like Ruth or Mary at school, well, mostly Mary, they accepted me.

She gave me the third degree at first, like Mr Merris in Maths, and I had to produce my school library card to show I was not an imposter. But since then, we have got on very well, and I have even been to tea with her in her council flat.

It is on the 27th floor of a tower block and, contrary to what you might think, unlike the Empire State Building, there is no view to speak of. There are three great tower blocks on her estate in an otherwise empty space with absolutely nothing in between—like a stage set. I would not have been surprised if Tyrannosaurus Rex had strolled out from between them.

Hamilton Terrace, where Grandfather lives, is a pleasant street and, though quite near the estate, it is like a different world.

Grandfather and I have made a prison visit to see my father, and that is the reason I am writing to you. By the way, a prison visit is quite something. I don't suppose you have ever been on one, though Mrs Robinson—the lady who does for Grandfather—has, several times.

You get frisked with metal detectors, patted down, sniffed at by dogs, then you get one hour to talk. Surprisingly, there is a tea-bar where you can buy cake and tea.

The thing is, my father asked me to retrieve a small box for him. It is hidden away in the rafters of a sort of tenement off the Gray's Inn Road. There are some dodgy characters around, he said, and I should look out for myself. I thought it would be a good idea if I had someone with me to watch my back when I go in for it.

So, if you are happening down to London any time soon, I wondered if you would be my accomplice? I am not in touch with any of the boys from school at the moment or I would ask one of them.

Before we did the prison visit, we phoned Mrs Clarke at school— you know she is a JP—and she gave very good advice and sent me my student identity card. We would never have got in without it.

It seems the Headmaster and Mrs Clarke are all still there at school, so perhaps I could have stayed after all? The online schoolwork is going fine; we are all getting it done on time and it's OK, but without the fun of having the stick insects and chameleons brought in to Biology, or electrocuting boys in Physics, or blowing things up in Chemistry.

Let me know if you are in London at all and will be my back-up.

Spike Kingswell

I forgot to mention that Grandfather and I get on very well, and we are well looked after by Mrs Robinson, who stands no nonsense but is a very good cook.

I addressed the envelope, put a stamp on from Grandfather's box on his desk, and went off to pop it into the red pillar-box at the end of the road.

Chapter 16
Go For It!

I cycled over several times and dropped by to see the little bent old lady, Annie, in Room 4A of the tenement building, and together we started on a family tree for her. But she lost interest quite quickly and became apprehensive, even superstitious, about documenting all her family.

I ventured up the stairs a few times and found the key for Room 4 hanging on the inside of the door to the broom cupboard, but something always stopped me from going ahead and getting the job done. I was getting to know the times when Alf left to go to his job handing out the evening papers.

At last, there came a time when I entered the lobby and neither Annie nor Eric had their doors open, and I judged I would be free to get up to the top floor without being seen or heard. It was a bit later than my usual time. I put the bicycle over the fence into the little grassy area of the park and laid it flat on its side. I went back into the lobby and up the stairs as quietly as I could and opened the broom cupboard door.

It was a bit darker than previously. My heart thumped as I felt for the key. If it was hanging there, the room would be empty and I should go ahead. My hands met the large cold key. It was hanging there, and I unhooked it and took it out to the landing, softly shutting the broom cupboard door behind me. If I was going to do it at all, it had to be now.

It was already dusk, and the stairs were in near darkness. I had not expected it to be quite so dark up here. Each room had a little window, but that let in very little light. I quietly inserted the key into the lock of the door of Room Number 4D. It turned easily with a click. I opened the door, slipped into the room, and shut the door behind me.

There was even less light here than on the landing, if that was possible, and so I stood for a moment to let my eyes acclimatise. I wondered if I should look for and find a light switch, but slowly my vision accommodated to the dim light. The ceiling was low on this top floor and I had only to reach up above the lintel of the door to find the space under the eaves.

As I waited to let my eyes get used to the semi-darkness, I cast my eyes around the room—and froze. Appalled. Terrified at what I saw. I was shocked by the sudden realisation that I was not alone. Across the room, sitting up cross-legged on the bed and staring at me with enormous round eyes, was a very small person. I thought my heart would stop.

'Hello!' I said hoarsely. The small person did not move. Nor speak.

'Hello!' I said again, speaking softly so no one else in the building was disturbed. 'I've just come to fetch my things!'

I reached up over the lintel of the door and my hand met with something that might well have been the box that I was looking for. Taking it down and thrusting it into my pocket, I checked again, and there was a second, smaller box which I also took and put in the pocket on the other side. My hand swept the space again, but there was nothing else there.

'All done!' I said reassuringly in a sing-song voice and nodded to the apparition, who continued to stare with her large round eyes, unmoving. I backed out of the room as quietly as I could. He or she made no move to follow me.

I felt I must lock the door again and replace the key correctly, though every extra minute I spent there risked being discovered. I locked the door and hung the key back in its place. Quietly, I pulled the broom cupboard door to and crept down the stairs again.

I was trembling by the time I reached the last step and regained the floor of the lobby, shaken still by the unexpected sight of the little doll-like person. I was about to congratulate myself that I had pulled it off when I thought I glimpsed, through the dusk, the shadow of a bulky figure on the far side of the cobbled street.

I paused in the lobby. At least I was standing in darkness and could not be seen. Perhaps I was imagining it. My nerves were so stretched that my mind might have registered an imaginary shadow. But at that moment, a bus went down the Gray's Inn Road, shedding transmitted light down the length of the cul-de-sac, and I could transiently see that the shadow was no trick of my imagination. One of the two heavies was leaning against the wall on the opposite side, can of Red Bull in his hand, just lounging.

There was no way I was going to risk walking out with that chap out there and have the metal boxes taken off me. They hung heavy in my pockets. I slunk back into the shadows of the lobby and tucked myself into the small space behind the staircase, by the sink and the half door to the toilet, and waited.

After a time, I felt my knees buckle and I slid down in the gap so that I was crouching under the sink and beneath the staircase. I waited again. After a time, I felt ready to nod off as I sat crunched up in the borderline between sleep and waking, my head on my knees. I was prepared to sit it out and see what happened and simply bide my time until it was safe to come out.

Time passed. And after a while, I even nodded off. I did not know how long I had been sitting there.

I came to with a jerk at the noise of Alf returning home from his evening job of handing out the newspapers. The heavy came across and accompanied Alf into the lobby. The two men spoke together and seemed on friendly terms. The footsteps of both men thundered aloft, up the stairs, shaking the wooden structure over my head as the two men clambered up, with me crouched below them in the gap under the staircase.

I heard the Heavy say, 'I've brought your little one a present. How's she doing? Any better?' and Alf replied, 'She's just the same. She's never going to get any better.'

Then I heard they were taking the key from the broom cupboard and, in a trice, they would be unlocking the door and into the top-floor room. Who knew what the spooky little cross-legged figure would convey to them, and who knew what they would find missing—if they were aware of the storage of items above the lintel of the door under the gables. I was just relieved that I had taken the time to re-lock the door and hang the key back in its proper place.

I unfurled myself from the cramped position under the stairs, slipped out of the lobby and into the cobbled street and, in a trice, vaulted over the fence into the park—all in less than a few seconds. But they may have heard a noise, as I thought I heard the Heavy call out, 'What was that?!'

By then, I had seized my bike and shot off around the gravel paths of the park, my heart pounding, pedalling as fast as I could go through the small green space. There was almost no one still remaining in the park. I was relieved that the gates still stood ajar.

I had to wait to cross to the other side of the main road before threading my way uphill between buses and cars, pedalling vigorously up the Gray's Inn Road, my heart pounding. I was relieved to find myself soon lost to view amongst the rumble of heavy traffic around King's Cross.

I felt safe once there were plenty of buses and cars, and, being on a bike, I could weave in and out of the vehicles and wasn't held up where cars had to slow and queue in a traffic jam, waiting for traffic lights to change.

Grandfather was in the kitchen making himself a goodnight drink of Horlicks as I wheeled the bike across the hall, leaving the customary wet tyre marks across the tiles. Grandfather called out to offer to make me a drink and I thanked him—but not Horlicks, I said—warm milk would be fine, with ideally a spoonful of chocolate powder stirred in.

The heaviness of the retrieved metal boxes was dragging down the pockets of my jacket, and I hastily stuffed both items into the top of Alicia's box, which lay, still un-sellotaped, at the back of the hall, before joining Grandfather in the kitchen.

We said our goodnights, and as Grandfather went to lock the front door, I took the hot chocolate upstairs. It was late.

Mission achieved for my father.

Chapter 17

Gone Fishing

There was a flurry of schoolwork online to get the syllabus finished before the half-term break, when no work would be set for a week.

I received another letter with the strong slanting handwriting in turquoise ink and the Scottish stamp, addressed to S. Kingswell, and this time I shared the contents with my grandfather.

'Grandfather, I've had another letter from my Housemaster, Mr Benson, and he's asked me if I'd like to stay with him in his sister's house for a week over the Bank Holiday and the half-term week.'

'Would you like to go?'

'I would like to. It would be interesting to see his sister's house. I've never been to Scotland. But would you be alright on your own?'

Grandfather gave a wry smile. 'I lived on my own here for years, Spike, before you came,' he reminded me. 'But yes, I will miss you. You're no trouble!' he added.

'That's what I said to Mrs Robinson—that I was no trouble—and she said it was very, very good of you to take me in and I should be grateful! But it's difficult for me to imagine your living here without me.'

With that, Grandfather actually laughed, not a common occurrence. 'It's difficult for me to imagine also. All things considered, I've enjoyed your staying here, and I hope that when your school reopens and you go back, you'll feel able to say that you always come here to your grandfather's for the holidays. Now, how do you plan to get to Scotland? It's more than four hundred miles. Train or coach, I should think. Coach would be cheaper, but it's a long, wearisome way. The train journey is quicker and quite interesting, and if you book a window seat on the right-hand side as you go north, there are wonderful views of the coastline and castles. And of course, you can have a meal on the train. It's about five hours on the train. I'm happy to pay for the train ticket if that's what you decide. You'll need to ask your Mr Benson about the connections once you get to Scotland.'

'Thank you, Grandfather. Perhaps we could book it online together. Now—shall we book return or single? That way I'll know if you're really happy to have me back!'

Grandfather smiled again. 'We'll make it return! If you're happy, I'll just check with the Clarkes that they are agreeable for you to go—the school likes to know where you are—and I can give them the address, if I may.'

I handed over the letter to Grandfather for him to make a note of the address.

We decided on a train leaving King's Cross at half past nine in the morning, which got into Edinburgh just after lunch—2:15—a time that suited the Housemaster to meet the train. We booked just the ideal seat that Grandfather had recommended: facing forward, a window seat with a table, on the right so that I would be on the coastline side, and near the dining car.

The anticipated views from the train window met all expectations.

The Housemaster had said he would meet me at the station, and there he was on the platform with three other boys from our House. We did not, in fact, go to the sister's house at all. His sister apparently had made it clear that she could do with a break from her brother's continual presence, and when she found her brother had offered to have no fewer than four boys from his House for half-term, she suggested he take them for a fishing holiday in the Highlands. She had a friend with a small cottage in Tomintoul who was willing to lend it, and Mr Benson had agreed enthusiastically and set about making the arrangements.

Tomintoul was one of several small villages in the Cairngorms that all claimed to be the highest village in Scotland. When I got off the train, there was my Housemaster and the other boys from his House, and we all set off together, packed into Mr Benson's car. It was late when we arrived at the cottage—up a rough track and some way out even from the village—and in dense darkness.

We had to search in the dark for the key to the door of the cottage and found it eventually under a stone to the right of the front step: a large, featureless iron key, which opened the door. We were met by further complete darkness within. We all tumbled into the one large room. We found a light switch and blinked in the sudden illumination.

If it was cold outside in the night air, it was equally cold inside the living room. The cottage was fairly basic, with wooden untreated floors and shutters—no curtains.

One of the boys was volunteered by Mr Benson to make a fire in the open hearth, just to take the chill off the room, and the rest of us all set to and helped to carry in the huge cardboard carton with the supplies for the week and unpack the provisions, while Mr Benson made a start at cooking what he said was his speciality dish: spaghetti bolognese.

We put the provisions onto the shelves and were interested to see what he had brought: milk and oats—porridge was also his speciality, he claimed—brown sugar for the porridge, vast numbers of eggs, bacon and sausages, tomatoes, a big bag of large potatoes, a bag of apples, two huge loaves of bread, butter, jam and marmalade, tea, some tins and yet more spaghetti.

The water, when it gushed out of the single tap to fill the kettle and the saucepan, was icy cold.

Once the fire was going and the stores unpacked, we boys were all sent up to claim our bunk beds and lay out our sleeping bags while Mr Benson made good progress cooking his speciality dish – the spaghetti bolognese – which was exactly what was wanted at the end of the day. One boy, who was younger and smaller than the rest of us, said he would just climb into his sleeping bag and go to sleep, foregoing any food, but Mr Benson was having none of that. He hauled him down to eat with the rest of us before he could nod off, and once the food was set before him, he tucked in like all the rest and got his second wind. We all agreed the speciality dish was absolutely first class – and nothing was left over.

'For the rest of the week,' our Housemaster declared, 'you'll need to catch enough trout to feed us all. We'll fry them gently and eat them with bread and butter.'

'I've never caught a fish,' said one.

'Perhaps I should have said we'll need to catch enough trout so that we don't all go hungry.' He gestured to the rods. 'I hope you're all going to be proficient fishermen.'

In the corner of the sitting room stood a stack of fishing rods, the canes leaning together propped against the wall, their tangled cords rattling in the breeze whenever the door was opened. A posse of waterproof anoraks and Berber jackets hung on a row of wooden pegs behind the door. Wellington boots in various sizes stood in pairs beneath the coats, some upright, others with the tops flopping sideways, tired out from communal use, the odd thick sock protruding from the mouth.

'Another evening we'll light the fire earlier and get the place warmer, but I think tonight we'll just eat and then get some sleep.'

The spaghetti bolognese had been truly excellent—very filling and just what was needed. We had all had enough.

'Before we go up,' Mr Benson said, 'I want you all to come and step outside, just for a moment, boys, and see the night sky.'

It was cold—very cold.

Outside the front door, the darkness was dense, impenetrable, unsullied by lights. The night sky was studded with stars.

'We'll have a proper look another evening, but the night sky is quite different without the reflected lights of the city. I hope you've brought plenty of sweaters and warm things,' Mr Benson said. 'Pile them all on and climb into your sleeping bags. Another night, I'll have two volunteers for washing up, but tonight you can all get to sleep.'

'No, we'll give you a hand and help wash up.'

I and two others at once stayed to help, and we sent the young chap up to get his sleep. But then we needed no further encouragement. We all needed our rest as we embarked on the strenuous, demanding week ahead.

The streams teemed with brown trout, young and old, and we four boys and our young Housemaster tramped up and down the edges of the streams, through the tall wet grass, in various-sized welly boots, plying the rods under the reeds and into the recesses under the banks where the trout lurked. We jerked the rods when a fish took the bait to secure it on the hook, wound it in, and landed it on the grass behind us—chasing through the long, wet grass to find where it had landed, stunning it, and adding it to the pile. We learned to wind the tackle, handle the hooks and bait, the floater and the weight.

Back inside the cottage, we gutted the fish onto newspaper and washed them under the single cold tap that gushed icy fresh water. We fried them softly in butter, grilled them, or roasted them on an open fire, and—to be honest—we were getting a little tired of eating trout by the end of the week.

In the evenings, we sat by the open fire, played cards, and talked, and once the flames were dwindling to glowing ashes in the grate, we added no more logs but went off to bed.

For one day, we were let off from trout fishing and Mr Benson took us all to Aberdeen. We explored the port, fed by the rivers Dee and Don and opening out onto the cold North Sea. We climbed up onto the Torry Battery to look down on the harbour and view the ships from the heights, and we spotted seals basking on the banks.

We enjoyed the Zoological Museum of the University of Aberdeen, where Mr Benson had an admission card because he had studied there. It was full of amazing large skeletons from prehistoric times. We had no time to go on to see the Maritime Museum and saw only the outside of the Tolbooth Museum, which was an old converted prison.

'Maybe another time,' he said. It was home country to Mr Benson, as he had grown up in the area, and he pointed out to us the grey stones of the city buildings, all built from granite dug out from the works outside the city.

'Aberdeen's the Granite City,' he said.

On that one day off from trout fishing, we went to the shops in Aberdeen for more milk and bread and bought lamb chops and steak to take 'home' with us to cook in the cottage—a welcome change from the trout. Then we sat around in the fug of the open fire in the hearth, which warmed one's front but less efficiently one's back, and somehow never quite took the chill off the whole room.

We thankfully nestled down into our padded sleeping bags, knowing full well that we would all wake with the early dawn as soon as the morning light came through the unshuttered windows, to be followed by yet another day in the wet countryside by the trout streams.

On our last evening, we sat round the fire with blankets around our shoulders and played a game where we all related the most interesting thing we had done in the weeks since school had closed.

The most unusual thing that I had done, of course, was to visit my father in Wormwood Scrubs prison, but there was no way I was ready to share that with the other boys—though I had told my Housemaster all about it in a letter.

Instead, I told of my visit to retrieve the metal box from where it had been hidden under the rafters of a house. I told the story vividly, reliving again my exploits: how I had put my borrowed bike over the wall into the park to make good my escape, going up to the empty room—empty as I had thought—and finding the sought-after metal box, but being horrified by the presence of an apparition in the room.

I made it sound like a ghost, and they all listened, enthralled, as I told them how I had seized the box and fled with it—down the stairs and out into the alleyway, putting one hand on the wall at the end of the street and vaulting over it, grabbing my bike, and riding away. I only mentioned the one box and didn't say too much about hiding in the cubbyhole under the stairs until the coast was clear for fear of the Heavies—in fact, I didn't mention that at all. Instead, I focused on weaving my way through the traffic around King's Cross on the borrowed bike.

The others listened to my story, rapt. They were not sure what to make of it. They demanded to know at once what was in the box. I had to admit lamely that I didn't know. They looked at me with suspicious, unbelieving eyes. It did seem extraordinary—even to me now—that I had been so lacking in curiosity about what was in the box. But it was so. Once I had retrieved the box, I had felt 'mission accomplished'.

That did not satisfy the boys, and they began to express their doubts about my whole story. I thought about how I could convince them. I did remember then—something I had forgotten all about—that I had picked up a tiny key. So, putting my hand now deep into my pocket, I fished out the little key. It was quite ornate, with little engraved wings on the handle. They handed it round the circle. It added some support to my extraordinary tale.

They asked then where the box was now. I was struck with a sudden concern for the safety of my little box. How could I have been so forgetful? So much had happened since—what with the half-term holiday and the planning of going up to Scotland, the fishing and the camaraderie of the group—that the whereabouts of my rescued treasure had completely slipped my mind. I said I had dumped it somewhere in my grandfather's house. I couldn't say that it was in my grandfather's estranged daughter's box of possessions from her past. That was too fanciful. So I just admitted that I hadn't opened it yet and that I would look into it when I got back. My story finished rather lamely.

One of the boys said, 'I didn't know you had a grandfather.'

I could answer that. 'I didn't know I had either—until this epidemic crisis. I found him then, and we get on okay together.'

'I'm glad for you,' said the Housemaster, taking over. 'Actually, we all have—or had—two grandfathers. And two grandmothers, for that matter. Four grandparents and two parents. None of mine are still alive—neither grandparents nor parents. So I just have a sister.'

'I thought we were going to stay with her,' I said.

'So what happened?' said one of the other boys.

'Once she heard you were coming, she changed her mind!' said the wit amongst the boys. We all laughed. A small spasm crossed the Housemaster's face—a wince—followed by a look of sadness.

'Something like that,' he said.

None of the other boys had as exciting a story to tell as I. But on the other hand, all the other boys had a home and a family to go to, which counted for a lot, I felt.

All of us boys were enjoying ourselves hugely on this half-term holiday, and hopefully our Housemaster was too. But increasingly I was beginning to worry about the whereabouts of the metal boxes, realising that I should never have placed them in Alicia's box of things in the first place—and regretting even more that I had not retrieved them at once while I could. I should have moved them to a place of safety. In fact, I should have extracted them the very next day and hidden them somewhere else.

Somehow, once I had achieved my father's mission—the rescue of the box—some of the concerns about it had disappeared from my mind. I had not even been that curious about its contents. And of course, I had the other little box too, which I had picked up inadvertently alongside it. I was not even sure which was the intended box.

I put the small ornate key back into my trouser pocket. I wondered which box, if either, would be opened by it. I patted the inside pocket of my jacket to reassure myself of the presence of the return ticket tucked into the innermost pocket. I was looking forward now to going home, back to Maida Vale. I recognised that this was a new sensation for me—a longing to get back home.

On the last day, we tidied up the cottage, put the large iron door key back under the stone by the door, and piled into Mr Benson's car. Right up to the last moment, I wondered whether we might yet get to see the house in the Highlands where my Housemaster had been brought up and where he had been staying, and whether we might get to meet his sister. Seeing the house and meeting the sister would have somehow extended my feeling of belonging and kinship.

It was not to be. We were all to be deposited at the station to take the train journey back.

As we stood together on the station platform at midday, waiting for our train to come in and take us away, Mr Benson asked if we had enjoyed ourselves.

For sure, this was our cue to thank our Housemaster, and we did so in varied ways. He asked us all what we planned to say in the account that we were surely going to have to write for school about how we had spent half-term.

'I shall say, it was very cold. I shall say that I shall never forget how cold it was. There was nothing you could do really to get warm. Then, to sit by the fire with the crackling logs in the evening was really nice. But you still had to leave it to go and get into your sleeping bag.'

'And the dark. The cold and the dark. The dark was incredible. That blackness without streetlights is so dense. You just can't see a thing. And that does mean you can see the stars properly. I'd never seen the stars quite like that before. You could imagine seeing them like that if you were Ancient Man or if you were a sailor, and would orientate and steer by the stars. They were brilliant.'

'And we all learned to fish. I had never caught anything before. It is really amazing to eat what you have just caught—fresh fish. The trout was good.'

'Actually, Mr Benson, we all want to thank you for taking us along.'

We all nodded, and there was a chorus of murmurs of appreciation. 'We do. We do.'

'Did you enjoy it, Sir?' said the wit.

He looked us over. 'I did,' he said. 'It was splendid. And you were all splendid. You were really good company—good sports.'

'What are you going to do now, Sir?' asked another.

'I am just going off to my sister's, and probably I shall sleep for—maybe twelve hours, maybe twenty-four hours, maybe even longer.'

Chapter 18

I've Lost the Boxes

The train from Edinburgh to King's Cross got in in the late afternoon, and I caught a bus along the Euston Road westward, then walked the short distance from the bus stop north up to Maida Vale, my backpack slung over my shoulder. As I trudged up the familiar avenue, with the plane trees down the centre of the road, my heart lifted—home—and I greeted the wisteria over the front porch with a smile, like meeting up with an old friend.

Grandfather was snoozing in his leather armchair in the study when I walked in. He had left the door on the latch for me.

I dumped my pack on the ground and put a hand on Grandfather's shoulder.

'I'm back,' I said.

Grandfather opened his eyes.

'So I see. Welcome home. Did you have a good time?'

'I did. We did. But we didn't go to his sister's house. I think she's had enough of him. There were three other boys from our

House at school, and Mr Benson took the four of us trout fishing. We went to a village called Tomintoul—it claims to be the highest village in Scotland—and we stayed in a stone cottage that was outside even the village. We fished for trout every day in the streams. Actually, I've brought some trout back. I'd better put them in the fridge, unless you want to eat them tonight. We had a great time.'

'That's good. I think put them in the fridge. Mrs Robinson has prepared something for tonight. Are you tired? We can eat early. Do you want to go and see what she's done for us?'

'I will. I see you've put the cardboard box back up into the loft— you know, the box that was at the back of the hall. I should have sellotaped it again and taken it back up the ladder for you before I left.'

'No. No need. Alicia came round again and took it away; she got a taxi and carried it off to her flat. She lives quite near, in Little Venice.'

My heart sank. The cardboard carton contained my two rescued metal boxes—and it had gone.

As we sat over our evening meal in the kitchen, I went very quiet. I worried.

'Grandfather, you're going to be very annoyed with me. I've done something stupid. I need to think through what I've done and how I can put it right.'

'Good gracious, Spike! I can't imagine you've done anything worrying. Tell me the problem and I'll see what can be done to put it to rights.'

'Can we discuss it in the morning, Grandfather?'

'I'd rather you told me now, Spike. I often find that if you have a problem and are worrying about it before you go to bed, if you think it over just before you go to sleep, when you wake up, your mind has solved it for you.'

'I hope that will work then. I stupidly slipped something into the cardboard box and I should have retrieved it at once before going away. I need to get it back,' I blurted out.

'Well, I don't see that's too much of a problem. We'll contact her and you can tell her what it is, and you can arrange to meet her and she'll give it back.'

He made it sound straightforward.

I was silent again.

'I feel nervous about meeting her.'

'Of course. And she is doubtless nervous about meeting you. So this will turn out to have been a convenient way of meeting for a purpose. It may be that, in the end, neither of you will want to take your acquaintance any further, but you will have met in a civilised way and can leave it at that. On the other hand, you may find that you like each other enough to form some sort of—what shall we say—friendship? It doesn't have to be a meeting of souls.'

'Do you really think she is as nervous about meeting me as I am about meeting her?'

'I certainly do, Spike. I am sure of it. She is still very young, you know. She has not had an easy upbringing. You can understand that, sharing a similar situation. But she has shed any unfortunate friends she made and is ready to build a new life.'

'Would you come with me, Grandfather?'

I looked at his wise old face while he thought that through. After a bit, he said,

'Do you know, I think it is something you have to do on your own, Spike. But I can help you with it. I'll phone her up and arrange the meeting for the handover of the— I've forgotten what it is—that you slipped into her box and want back.'

'It's a box. A metal box. Actually, two metal boxes.'

'Mysterious! It sounds like a spy story to me. I'm glad the trout fishing was after that, not before. If you'd popped a couple of fish into her box and left them there for a week, that would not have been a good idea.'

I smiled.

'Thank you, Grandfather. What would I do without you!'

It was good to be home.

Chapter 19

Open the Box

The handover was arranged. The meeting was set for a quarter past twelve midday on the canal bank in Regent's Park. There was a bench just before the Maida Vale tunnel where we were to meet.

So, just after twelve, I left Grandfather's house in Maida Vale, ducking under the wisteria blooms festooned over the porch, and started off walking down the avenue to my assignment. The plane trees that lined our street were beginning to cast their sticky burrs over the dry, crumbly soil that harboured the roots of the ancient trees. Hamilton Terrace was a pleasant street to live on. I tried not to think of the challenge churning in my mind—the choice that lay before me. I debated it with myself. I felt as though I were two people. Two different people. At any rate, I thought, I did have two choices.

At its simplest: *I am a schoolboy temporarily living with my grandfather while school is closed because of the virus epidemic, and I'm simply going to retrieve my property—the two small metal boxes that I stupidly went to hide, inserting them into the cardboard carton in the back of the hall. I could retrieve them, apologise for putting them in her carton, thank her, and go. And forget about the rest. That's one person.*

The other: *I am a fourteen-year-old young person going to meet a young woman whom I have never met before; she must be thirty-two years old now or so, and she and I have—had—the closest relationship that any two people can ever have. I should be brave enough to do more than just say hello.*

It was not far to go now. *I live in Maida Vale, she lives in Little Venice. And I am really nervous about meeting her.*

We arrived, walking towards the bench from opposite directions, at the same moment. Each of us felt it was a good omen that neither had kept the other waiting. We exchanged the simplest of greetings.

'Hi,' I said.

'Hello, Spike,' she answered.

I looked at the blue canvas bag she was carrying. It was a quality bag—heavy denim, with a brown leather carrying handle and leather strips reinforcing the corners.

'I expect you've brought along my boxes.'

'I have. I didn't know they were yours or I wouldn't have opened them. They were amongst my things, so I presumed they were mine.'

'You've opened them?' I said, astonished. 'What's in them?'

'Do you not know?' she said.

I shook my head.

'They were locked.'

I dove down into my trouser pocket and produced the little ornate key.

'This may, or may not, open one of them.'

'Goodness! A man of surprises!' she flattered me.

She held out her hand, palm up, and I placed the key in her hand. Our hands touched. She inspected the key and said at once,

'I think it will open one box but not the other.'

'But how did you open them?' I was genuinely puzzled.

'I used my artist's paraphernalia—a palette scraper and a crochet hook. The experience of ten years of dissolute living,' she laughed. 'Remember, I thought they were part of my gear from fourteen years ago, so I needed to open them to see what I had put in them.'

'Ten years of dissolute living. You don't look very dissolute.'

'I am an artist,' she said, then added, 'What do I look like?'

'You look beautiful,' I said, jokingly, feeling myself won over, and remembering Grandfather's words when she came to the door and I had glimpsed her briefly.

'What shall I call you?' I asked.

'Alicia,' she said.

We sat on the bench in the sunshine with the blue canvas bag between us. She took out the two metal boxes and laid them on the bench alongside. She handed the small key back to me.

'I think the smaller box,' she said. 'The other is surprisingly heavy.'

The key fitted like a dream and the lid clicked open. A film of protective tissue paper lay on top. Then, photographs. Too many to take out and look through on a towpath bench. Beneath them, money notes.

'What do you want to do?' she said. 'I don't think you can go through the contents sitting here in wind and sunshine. Do you want to come back to my flat and go through them properly? I can explain what I think some of them are. And I can open the other box for you. I think the other one may be nothing to do with you or me. Or, if you prefer, we can go to your grandfather's—my father's—house.'

'I haven't told Grandfather how or why I have got the boxes. Or even that there are two. So we'll go back to your flat, if that's OK? To explain: I went to get a box from a hidden place in a near-derelict property and found there were two boxes, and so I took them both, not knowing which was the one I was meant to collect.'

We closed the lid, and she gathered up both boxes into her blue canvas bag to carry them. I had meant to say I was sorry to have put my things into her carton of possessions, and to apologise, but the moment to say that had gone by.

We made our way into the Maida Vale tunnel, plunging into sudden relative darkness as the tunnel cut off the sunshine.

'I always look carefully around to see who is lurking about before I enter this tunnel,' she said.

We emerged on to the Little Venice side of the canal. Along the canal were the moored barges where people made their homes and lived. She pointed up to the balcony of one of the buildings that lined the street.

'That's the balcony of my flat. We'll go on up.'

She went at once to unlock and open the glass doors to the balcony, and fresh air flooded in.

'I have an amazing outlook,' she said. 'Go through and have a look.'

I went on to her balcony and stood briefly amongst her plants, looking down on the canal scene and barges below. What a view! I looked back into her flat. Her room possessed a quiet, reassuring atmosphere. I was no expert in household things or arrangements, but I felt everything in the uncluttered space had been chosen in the best possible taste.

She set the two metal boxes down on a small table, and I took the chair next to it and opened the smaller of the two metal boxes with the key. I hardly knew where to begin. She had gone over to her kitchen area and was pouring apple juice into two tall glasses, adding ice cubes to float in them. She laid the glasses on two small coasters on the breakfast bar.

'Do you want to bring the little box up here and lay out the contents on the surface? We can try and make sense of them. I'll probably be able to identify one or two of them, but the others will be a mystery to me. Hopefully, for those I don't recognise, you will be able to tell me who and what they are.'

We sat opposite each other on the high stools, either side of the breakfast bar, and sipped the apple juice. I carefully took off the small layer of protective tissue paper, followed by a small stack of photographs. She went to draw the curtains halfway across her balcony windows to lessen the sunlight streaming in.

I laid the first photograph down on the surface of the bar.

She smiled. 'I know that one! That's me at seventeen,' she said. 'A schoolgirl. That's the only one of me, and you can see that I've changed!'

She put it to one side. I picked it up. I supposed she was not much older than I was now when that was taken—perhaps two or three years older, only.

She said again, 'That's the only one of me.'

She picked up the next photograph. 'And this is your father at about the same time. When you've looked at it, put it aside, if you will. And look at it later. I don't want to dwell on it for now. But for the rest, you'll probably identify and recognise them better than I can.'

Was that really my father? I thought. Well, I could see that it could be, but of course, I wouldn't recognise him now. As she requested, I put it to one side.

I began to turn the rest over slowly.

'Pat and Tony,' I said, laying the next one down.

There they stood, as I remembered them best. Two stalwart people.

'I thought it must be,' Alicia said. 'Your father's parents. I'm quite interested to have you identify them for me. But—look—stop, if it upsets you.'

I tilted up my face to look at her. 'I'm quite resilient,' I said.

Then—baby, toddler, small boy—lots of snaps of me doing the sort of things small children do. There was nothing to say. We both looked through the pictures of me throughout my childhood. Some toys I recognised. Some bikes.

A nice one of me with Pat. 'This is a really nice one of Pat and me.' I spent some time looking at it. 'She has died, you know,' I explained.

Then, Pat and Tony, looking older. Pat, not looking well. I could mull over them repeatedly later.

Then myself, still in short trousers, smart in a school blazer just before I went to Ranford School. I remembered my father's words:

Pat, I want him to look smart—school blazer, white shirt, school tie, long grey socks. And then my father's words again: *Stand up straight, shake hands with the Headmaster, call him Sir.*

And then—it stopped.

We sat in silence.

'This collection,' I said. 'It's not for me, nor for Grandfather—though I will show him them later. He is such a wise old man!—but they're not for me, nor for you. They're for my father, of course.'

I put them back together again, in order.

'And below all this,' said Alicia, 'is a stack of money. We should count it and make a note of the amount. It is not my business to tell you what to do with this money, but I will offer you a shrewd observation. After my life of dissolute living—*not really, that was just a joke*—and not a very good joke, let me start again: LIFE. If you have a little money behind you, LIFE is transformed. It is enabling. Money. It gives you choices.'

We counted it together and made a solemn record for each of us as to the amount. To me, it was a surprisingly large sum. I looked at her.

'What do you think?' I said.

Alicia advised me to put all the money shortly into a reputable savings account that offered both interest and instant access whenever it was wanted or needed—and to put it under my own name.

She explained, 'As you are underage, and as we are not sure whether this money is actually yours, it needs to go into the sort of savings account where no questions will be asked if you want or need to take some out. That's my opinion. That's what I think your father would want.'

'Thank you, Alicia,' I said. 'There's a lot to think about.'

I packed the first box together again, carefully putting everything back in.

She said, 'I'm going to make a suggestion. I'll open the second box in a minute, but let's take a break. Stand up, stretch, walk around.'

I agreed. We both got up and moved around a bit. I went to her balcony and opened the curtains again. They were heavy, green-patterned curtains, which slid open smoothly on their runners.

'They're the nicest of William Morris patterns,' she said. 'Printed on heavy linen and lined.'

I stood on the balcony and looked over at the barges and the people who lived on them. Her flat did have an amazing view. Her room was well organised with a calm atmosphere. Her artists' gear was stacked neatly in one corner.

'Before we look in depth at the contents of the second box, I suggest we have something to eat.' She had set about putting food out and pouring more apple juice into the glasses.

Along the breakfast bar from us was a pristine white envelope addressed to her, Miss Alicia Kingswell. A neat leather and silvery metal letter opener lay on top of it, and I picked it up without meaning to intrude. I saw that the envelope beneath it had the letterhead of Ranford School in the corner. The letter opener, like all the possessions in her flat, was of fine quality.

She nodded towards the letter. 'That's the letter from Ranford School that came out of the blue, telling me 'they were closing and Sebastian would be sent home!' Naturally, I thought it was a mistake. To be honest, Spike, I haven't given the past much thought.' She laughed. 'I even had some crazy picture of a toddler outside, not being able to reach up to the door knocker! I nearly threw the letter away. Then I thought I'd just phone the school and tell them about their mistake, and I found myself having a ridiculous conversation with Mrs Clarke, the Headmaster's wife, who kept telling me not to worry. I tried to tell her that I wasn't worrying and hadn't worried for years, and she kept telling me I was not to worry and that you were very enterprising.'

We both laughed. I could imagine Mrs Clarke's determination to get her points across. Alicia had set two plates before us—crusty bread, pâté, and a little salad—and topped up the apple juice in our glasses. We ate companionably without further talking.

The second box, which she skilfully opened with her artist's tools, was full of coins, and that was what made it so heavy. But they were not coins of the everyday currency, nor were they all the currency of the realm. I handled one or two. To be honest, they held little interest for me.

'Do you think this is a box you were also meant to pick up, or do you think you've picked up an additional box that actually belongs to somebody else? Someone who was hiding it away— some booty that may just be theirs, and that's where they secrete it, that's how they deal with it. It may have originally been stolen. It may have been forgotten. Or do you think the two boxes belong together? What do you think?'

'To be honest,' I said, 'I haven't the faintest idea. But I do know where we can get an opinion on the coins. A friend at Ranford, my school, is a coin collector—that's his hobby—and I went with him to Charing Cross Road once, where he was selling one coin that he had in duplicate in order to buy another to add to his collection. I sat on a stool in the corner of this mart while he did his transaction, and it was an amazing place.'

'Won't they be shut now, with the virus epidemic?'

'Maybe not. Or not yet. He probably lives there, over the shop. We could try tomorrow.'

'Do you want me to come with you?'

'Definitely. If you're free. I need someone with me. People buying coins there—sometimes they come in with a bodyguard. I've got to do my online lessons from school first, but we should get it done tomorrow. And if we can, can we deposit the money as you suggest?'

I took the smaller metal box home with me, along with the little key, and left the larger one with Alicia, having agreed that we would take it together to the Gold Coin Exchange shop.

We both stood up and each raised our right hand, allowing them to tap briefly together in a moment of agreement—not a clasping of hands, not a handshake, just a loose connection, keeping our distance, before I went on my way. It was enough.

Chapter 20
Relationships

I was carrying secrets now from all those people closest to me. There were too many of them—too many people—crowding out my thoughts, all sharing different parts of a knotty situation.

I was suddenly tired. I felt the weight on my shoulders.

I felt weary as I reached home.

It was the first thing Grandfather asked when I returned.

'How did it go? How did you get along?'

'It was fine, Grandfather.'

I would have shown the photographs and shared them with Grandfather, and I planned to do so in the future, but some instinct made me reluctant to do so until I had deposited the money—the notes that had lain beneath the photoprints—safely into a savings bank.

'It was fine,' I repeated. 'It was as though I had known her all my life.'

'What did you call her?' asked Grandfather, remembering the debate on this.

'Alicia,' I said. 'I asked her.'

I was suddenly tired with the tension I had faced meeting with Alicia. It had been such a momentous step. I had not sorted it out in my mind yet.

Later, as we had supper together, Grandfather reminded me to write and thank my housemaster for the week's trout fishing at half-term.

'Please don't delay. A thank-you letter should go off right away, as soon as you're back.'

'I would like to have met his sister and seen their house.'

Grandfather said, 'The ingratitude of schoolboys! It won't have cost him nothing to rent the cottage, ferry you around, feed you all four for a week, and drive to Edinburgh to collect you and take you back there at the end of the half-term.'

I shrugged.

Grandfather spoke again, rather acerbically, 'Spike, I hold these courtesies as very important. Please let me know when you have done it. I am perfectly happy to write and thank him myself if you're finding it a difficult task.'

This was the first occasion when Grandfather and I had had sharp words, had even almost fallen out.

I realised that Grandfather had been concerned as he waited anxiously to hear how my meeting with Alicia had gone—a meeting that he had helped to arrange—and hours had passed. I became aware that Grandfather was feeling excluded, even a little snubbed. He had such good manners. He had an exquisite reluctance to intrude on the sensitivities of others, not to invade sensitive feelings. He had held back, not to ask for more details than I could bring myself to share. I knew that I had not been very forthcoming with details about the day. I had not got my own emotions sorted out for myself and was not ready to embark on discussing them with anyone else.

Mrs Robinson had left us a pleasant meal, and there was a rhubarb crumble to follow with custard. We ate in near silence. Neither of us had much to contribute. As soon as he had eaten, Grandfather went and sat in his easy chair and closed his eyes. He had a small notebook and pencil with him and occasionally wrote a word or two. Then he closed his eyes again and was lost in deep thought.

I washed the dishes, left them to drain, put the food away, and then went and wrote my thank-you letter and put a stamp on it for posting. Before I went to say goodnight to Grandfather, I went to tell him that I had written a nice letter thanking Mr Benson and saying how much I had enjoyed the week. 'Best half-term ever,' I had written.

'Sorry if I'm unsettled, Grandfather. I've written the letter and thanked Mr Benson, and I will post it tomorrow. I found life easier in the past, you know, when I had nobody—just school. And school is very good. I can manage that. But now I have too much. I have you and Mrs Robinson here. I have Mr Benson as housemaster. And I nearly met his sister as well. And my father in prison. And now there is Alicia. We got on alright. But—she can't be—can't be—anything to me, you know.' I winced as I came to the word. 'I don't even like to think the word. It makes me shudder. I can't cope with that.'

'I can't say the word.'

'You don't have to,' said Grandfather. 'You don't have to. You really don't have to, Spike. Just look on her as a slightly older friend. Who, it turns out, happens to be a member of the family. Maybe not even like a big sister. Better, I think, like a cousin.'

'That's helpful, Grandfather. I'll look on her, as you say, as a cousin. A recent acquaintance that I have just realised is possibly a distant cousin. Someone I've come across by chance who just turns out to be, possibly, a relative.'

Grandfather changed the subject. 'Thanks for doing the letter, Spike. It probably means a lot to the housemaster. Other people have troubles, you know.'

'They do. He told us one evening in the cottage that he had no grandparents and no parents living. No other relatives. Just his sister.

And he says she is finding it a bit much having her brother come to live with her in this epidemic.'

'You did very well today, Spike. Your meeting with Alicia. It wasn't easy. I'm proud of you.'

Chapter 21

The GPO and the Gold Mart

The General Post Office in Little Britain was open for business. We went together.

Alicia thought the main GPO the best place to go, being the most impersonal. It was better than a small branch office where questions might be asked. I took along my Student Identity Card and used the version giving my surname as Kingswell, which was how I thought of myself now. Those cards were proving very useful: first for the prison visit, now for the Post Office. I opened a National Savings Account and deposited all the money from the little box. I put the whole lot in. It was a relief to me that one thing was accomplished. I was given a passbook.

'Thank you for helping me do that, Alicia. I know it may not be my money. It may be my father's. From what I remember, he just said to retrieve the box. But we had to put it somewhere. We can't just leave it lying around as notes. He can always have it back if he needs it later.'

Alicia said nothing.

Then we were off to the Charing Cross Road. The street was in shadows, and when we reached the Gold Exchange Mart, it had all the sinister appearance of an old opium den.

'What a place!' she said.

We rang the bell, which gave a muffled peal inside the shop, and we heard shuffling and someone pottering along to the door. The rasp of iron bolts being shot across to open up shook the door frame. The old man who answered the bell was wizened and bent, with a strong cigarette smell about him. His spectacles hung below his nose, from which rheumy mucus dripped and was repeatedly wiped away with a silk handkerchief of deep red and blue paisley pattern. He retreated behind the counter.

Behind him, on the back wall, were stacked in rows dusty vermilion boxes, their leather covers worn and rubbed away, flaking off, all labelled with stamps of identification from the Royal Mint.

Alicia and I deposited the larger of the two metal boxes onto the old scored oak counter, and she opened the lid. There was no need to say anything. The absolute professional tipped out the coins onto a large padded mat, muttering their provenance as he recognised each, clicking his tongue against his teeth. He turned over one and then another, fingering the coins. He took his time. We waited in silence, propped up against the counter. At last, he spoke.

'A very nice collection,' he said in his old wavering voice.

He plucked out his polishing cloth and gave some selected coins a good going-over. He screwed a loupe into one eye socket, the better to inspect a coin or two.

'Their provenance?' he inquired.

'Found in an old property by chance,' Alicia said. 'My friend was picking up something else, and this was alongside.'

'I don't recognise it,' the old man said, 'so not recently stolen. Worth?' He got out a stubby pencil and started jotting down numbers on a pad as he turned over the coins with his thin gnarled fingers, stopping to give one an occasional polish with his cerulean blue chamois cloth. 'I need to check on one or two. I'll give you a credit receipt for them and leave them with me. I'll definitely buy these,' he swept a selection of some of them to one side, 'if you want to sell,' and, 'especially these,' he indicated a few amongst them. 'But give me a number of days, and I'll have them all checked out. I might take the lot.'

We both signed in as Kingswell, and I accepted the receipt.

'Leave the metal box with me too, if you will. I'll keep them all together in one place. You might eventually want to keep one or two that are interesting. Or let me know if there's something else in particular you want to buy.'

'We'll think it over,' said Alicia, and we were asked to come back in about five days. We thanked him and left. As we left, we heard the bolts slotted back in place after the street door was closed.

But by the time five days had gone by, London was entering a further, tighter, stricter control, and the old man's mart was in full lockdown, with him, my coins, and the large metal box all vanished inside the secure boarded front of his shop.

'At least we've deposited it somewhere safe,' I said. 'We have the receipt.'

'Let us hope so,' said Alicia.

'Well, I'm not sure whether it was ours to start with. The problem is, we don't really know whose it is. Now that all the money has been secured away, I can show Grandfather the photographs and tell him how I came to get the box. I like to be open with him.'

'And with me, I hope. Are you going to let me know how and why you got the box? You said your father had asked you to get and rescue it! You should know I haven't seen your father for fourteen years.'

I unburdened myself to Alicia. I found she already knew that Grandfather and I had visited my father in prison, but whether she had heard that from Grandfather or from Mrs Clarke, the Headmaster's wife at school, or both, I was not sure—maybe both. But I felt some relief in being able to tell someone of my father's words and his request to me to retrieve the box. That was the way my father had put it. He had given me some sort of address, and it had been quite a problem to work out exactly where the building was and locate the place. No, as far as I could remember, my father had only mentioned one box.

'With lockdown coming, I think I shall be permitted to continue visiting your Grandfather to bring food or a newspaper, though, of course, he has Mrs Robinson to do that for him. We'll see how we manage. Let me know if there's any problem. We'll see how it goes.'

***

When I got back, Grandfather handed me another letter that had come for him from my Housemaster and shared the contents with me. Mr Benson had written that it seemed Ranford School wanted him back now to help in organising the online work and streaming. He had permission to make the journey to return to school and would like to take the opportunity to stop by and call on us, meeting Grandfather at lunchtime while it was still allowed and before the shutdown came into full force. Grandfather was delighted at the prospect of meeting him, and Mrs Robinson was requested to prepare a suitable lunch.

Chapter 22

The Housemaster Passes Muster

Mr Benson, my Housemaster, had taken an early train from Scotland and arrived in Maida Vale in time for lunch.

Mrs Robinson had prepared a simple meal for the three of us: for me, my grandfather, and my Housemaster. She waited around, especially to greet Mr Benson and shake his hand. She clearly had the impression that this was some sort of school inspection and that there were standards to be met. Before she left us to sit and eat our lunch, she insisted on showing Mr Benson the study, which was also our sitting room, pointing out Mr Kingswell's desk and my small table where man and boy could sit and study and do our work. She drew his attention to the wall of books—a small library, she said. Then, she showed him my room and Grandfather's upstairs, demonstrating her pride in looking after us. Only then would she leave us to the meal she had prepared.

Later, she pronounced that she had found him very acceptable.

'Quiet,' she said, 'and no side to him. A very nice gentleman.'

Grandfather, too, found him agreeable, and they had a very good conversation over lunch. Grandfather expounded on his historical research into the effects that access to education had, both on the individual and on society in general, particularly in former times. Mr Benson discussed the ethos of Ranford School and the philosophy of learning beyond the curriculum when living in the community of a boarding school.

They were both thoroughly enjoying their discussion and looked as though they were set to continue for some time, so when they paused for breath at one point and when they had finished eating, I laid the small metal box on the table. Mr Benson raised his eyebrows, querying whether this was indeed the box. Grandfather learned for the first time that it was my father, at the time of the prison visit, who had surreptitiously made a request to me and given me instructions to retrieve the box. Grandfather was far from pleased to hear that and was unhappy that he had not been told of it before. The intrigue of the contents of the box was sufficiently interesting to draw attention away from too much dispute about it.

I produced the little ornate key and opened it up. The tissue paper layer was lifted, and the photographs were taken out, displayed, and explained. Grandfather and Mr Benson poured over all the pictures. Looking at them a second time, it struck me that I hadn't quite realised how poignant they were. They portrayed a lifetime—or the lifetimes of several people.

Grandfather laid the first two snaps down side by side.

'My daughter Alicia, fifteen years ago, and I presume this is Spike's father, both in their teens, though I never met him then, and he is unrecognisable from the man Spike and I visited in the prison. I can only look at them now with remorse and regret. It was a different time, of course, and attitudes have changed. I can't feel I come out of that time with any honour.'

They proceeded to the likenesses of Pat and Tony in the subsequent photographs—my childhood family, who had provided a home for me and brought me up. Neither Mr Kingswell nor Mr Benson had ever met Pat and Tony, and they were mildly interested to see the stalwart, solid pair who had brought me up. The snaps of me in babyhood and childhood carried less interest to either man.

When she saw them later, Mrs Robinson, however, poured over each and every one of them and was fascinated to see them, inspecting them closely and demanding full explanations.

Grandfather was tiring and left the table. He went and settled down in the study over a cup of coffee and said he would look again at the photos in the future if he might. Mr Benson had to be on his way to get to Ranford School.

'Don't get up, Mr Kingswell,' Mr Benson said. 'I must be on my way.'

They shook hands warmly, and Mr Benson began expressing his thanks and approval, saying how good it was that Grandfather had welcomed me into his home and how particularly helpful it had been that he had enabled me to make the visit to the prison to see my father.

Grandfather responded in turn, saying that he realised now, particularly after seeing the collection of photographs and realising how treasured they had been, how remarkable it was that my father, only a teenager at the time, had been so determined to take ownership of the child he had fathered when his own daughter had backed away from any commitment. He said he reflected now that he had expressed his own opinion at that time that it was highly unlikely that the boy would really be in a position to shoulder the responsibility of the child he was so insistent on owning, and that he had apparently been determined and had managed it, albeit commandeering his own parents to shoulder the task. He had been wrong to doubt him, Grandfather said.

Mr Benson said, 'Thank you for lunch, it was good to meet you, and see where Spike has settled, and...' he added with a twinkle, 'And thank Mrs Robinson for me too, please. I didn't like to disabuse her that I was not here to do a schools' inspection visit, but please convey to her that she has definitely passed muster!'

I walked with Mr Benson down Hamilton Terrace and suggested that I would like him, my Housemaster, to meet Alicia before he left, if he had time. I told him she had said we could call in to see her on his way back to Ranford School. We used the walk for me to give Mr Benson the details of all the drama of collecting the box, the existence of the second metal box, and the contents of both. It was clear to him that the contents of that first box had seemed meagre. The retrieval of a small handful of family photographs seemed an inadequate reason for my father to have put me in some danger retrieving them, but he had been too sensible to raise questions at the lunch table.

As we walked together to Alicia's flat, I launched into a full explanation to my Housemaster. There was just enough time on our walk to bring him fully up to speed: I had picked up two boxes not knowing whether they belonged together, had tucked them into a cardboard carton of Alicia's things to hide them temporarily in Grandfather's house, and had stupidly forgotten to retrieve them before the half-term fishing holiday. I told him how reluctant I had been to meet Alicia at all, but it had not been as bad as I had feared. I related with admiration how Alicia had managed to open both locked boxes, as she had naturally assumed they were hers from the past and so she had known the contents before I did. We had met for the first time when I went to retrieve the boxes from her, and she had been enormously helpful in deciding what to do with the contents.

'I have not told Grandfather, but there was a large amount of money under the photographs. We suppose it is my father's. We have put it all into a savings account, and it would be there for him when he comes out. Well, we put it in my name, but what else could we do?'

'I can see why,' my Housemaster reflected. 'Just so long as you realise, I suppose, that it may be his if he wants it back when he comes out. On the other hand, he may be happy to let you have it, or have the use of it, for sensible things. But I'm glad you told me about it. Now, what about the other box?'

I launched into a description of Alicia deftly opening the boxes with her artist's palette scraper and a crochet hook.

'So clever. Ten years of the experience of dissolute youth,' she said. 'She does not look dissolute, of course. That's her little joke to explain how she didn't need a key to open a lock on a box. The key, by the way, belongs only to the small one with the photos and the money. And it was sheer chance that I found it. The heavy, larger one was full of ancient coins. We took them to the Gold Mart in the Charing Cross Road. I knew about that because I had been there once with a boy from school who collects coins. We have a receipt for them while they're being looked over.' I prattled on. It was a relief to tell someone not directly involved.

'As your Housemaster,' Mr Benson said, 'I am in loco parentis for you, and I hope that all the people who know about these boxes, the money, and the coins prove to be trustworthy and honest. Clearly, it's possible that the contents of either or both boxes have been obtained outside the law. Your father is, after all, in prison for fraud. I have not much experience of unconventional lifestyles. I do recall the School Bursar telling me of a father—not yours—who had come to settle the school fees, laying a suitcase on the counter before him and opening it to reveal an astonishing sight: neatly bound rolls of notes to pay for all five years of school fees, with the words, 'I only deal in cash.' It was like something in a film, the Bursar said, but it was not as unusual as one might imagine. It was far from uncommon to have fathers from abroad paying in that way. I do not know, of course, how your father had met his obligation to the school fees while his court case was pending.'

And neither did I. But I was grateful that he had. My father had, of course, brought a friend along with him, I remembered—a man who had driven us to school in his car, and whose name I did not know. He might have played a part in the transaction. Or he might not.

We walked on together, me talking away, Mr Benson listening and thinking deeply.

When we, I and my Housemaster, arrived at Little Venice, we walked along the side of the canal with the barges moored alongside. It is a lovely and picturesque spot. All in all, the place and the scene, Mr Benson said, were rather reminiscent of an ancient narrow street with balconies in the old parts of an Italian city. We stopped to look up at the balcony which I pointed out, and there she was, looking out for us, leaning out and waving—a beautiful young woman. She made a striking picture. Mr Benson was clearly impressed.

Alicia had left the door of her flat open for us and was busy flicking on the kettle. She came forward to be introduced.

'Alicia,' I said. 'This is my Housemaster, Mr Benson.'

She offered her hand.

'Rob Benson,' he said. 'It's good to meet you, Miss Kingswell.'

'Alicia, please.'

'Rob, then.'

They stood still, holding each other's hand, gazing at each other, lost for words. Their hands were no longer really in a handshake; it was as though they were experiencing a recognition that had come on them suddenly and unexpectedly. Both were searching for the right words, for something more to say. They dissolved into laughter. Then we all three began talking at once, me telling Alicia that my Housemaster was now fully briefed.

I left them to it, to try to rescue their conversation, and went on to the balcony to peer out at the barge people. I was fascinated by their lives and how they lived in the open air. I found it extraordinary that the boat people sat there on their canvas chairs, talking and reclining without any embarrassment, as if they were unaware of the possible inspection by anyone who walked by—separated by only a few feet from passers-by on the pavements. I lingered on the balcony.

When I came back inside, I found my Housemaster and Alicia drinking tea together. They were sitting in two easy chairs around the little low table.

She had got out her tea things, which, like all her possessions, were rather special and attractive: paired green dragon tea cups with a gold rim, with the dragons chasing each other around the outside of the cup. They were elegant and fragile bone china. They were refilling their cups from the teapot, which held a fragrant pale brown aromatic liquid.

'Do you want some tea, Spike?' they asked me.

I shook my head. 'No thanks. You know, I think I'll get back to Grandfather. I've filled in Mr Benson with all the details of where we've got to in our continuing story of the boxes. The point is, we don't really know whether the boxes belong together or not. We don't know whether they both belong to my father, or whether I've inadvertently picked up someone else's property, and then we don't know whether that other person actually rightfully owns the coins. I think, for the moment, we just have to let sleeping dogs lie. I think I'll wander back to Maida Vale and join Grandfather if that's alright with you.'

It clearly was.

Once again, I had found the space around me becoming crowded. Crowded with too many people, too many relationships to deal with. I was looking forward to the solitary quiet of Hamilton Terrace.

***

I was a bit shaken by all that was happening. It is a strange thing in life that sometimes, by chance, when two people meet, the time and the place, the other person and the situation, are all in harmony. Whether one calls it a *coup de foudre*, a clap of thunder, or a mutual recognition, both experience it as a moment of signal importance. So it seemed to be in that hour for Alicia and Mr Benson. Those two: Alicia Kingswell, an artist whose life circumstances had changed radically in the last few weeks, coming face to face with me, a schoolboy she had not met before and whose existence, fourteen years earlier, had derailed her life; and Rob Benson, a schoolteacher, who, as Housemaster of one of the Houses at Ranford School, had just reminded me that he stood *in loco parentis* to me.

I walked away from them both, along the pavement by the moored barges. The inhabitants there were anonymous, and their presence did not impinge on me.

The space around me was becoming crowded with people.

I needed to get back to Hamilton Terrace and the sanctuary of the largely silent presence of Grandfather. My Grandfather held himself distant from me, his grandson. He had a respect for the autonomy of other people, for me. He didn't invade my space.

Chapter 23

Mary Benson

Grandfather was on the phone as I walked back in the door. He beckoned me to come over and I heard him say,

'He has just come in. You can have a word with him.' Then, putting his hand over the receiver, he said, 'It's Mary Benson, Mr Benson's sister in Scotland. Apparently, he's left a folder with all his notes for the school tutorials behind, and she thinks he will need them.'

He handed the phone over to me and went back to sit in his chair.

I took the phone off him and said, 'Hello, Miss Benson. I was hoping to come and see you when we came up to Scotland at half-term. We had a lovely time in Tomintoul, and thank you very much for arranging the cottage for us. What has Mr Benson left behind?'

Then I said, 'Oh dear. Is it not possible to post them to him?' I listened while she explained how difficult that was. I said, 'I see. I can imagine there would be a hefty pile of folders and papers. And if your local post office is shut to business, that does look impossible.' More talk, then I said, 'Would you like me to come up and get them, and bring them down? I would like to have met you and seen where you live. I'll ask Grandfather if that's alright. I'll phone you back with the times.'

To my surprise, Grandfather seemed to accept the arrangement as a sensible one. Perhaps living with me for this last short time had left him open to unexpected things happening. Perhaps, too, he was not the most practical person when it came to arranging the exigencies of life. Together, we got down the Atlas and Directory to look for the route and transport from Edinburgh Waverley Station to her cottage in the Highlands. As far as we could see, I would need to go not to Edinburgh but either to Aberdeen or to Inverness, and then take a bus into the Highlands.

Mary Benson was not a great help as to which was the preferable rail terminal to try for; neither city seemed to have a plentiful bus or coach connection across the Highlands, preferring to creep round the coast like the local railways, rather than cut across the mountains of the Grampians. We booked the train to Scotland again, this time with an open return.

Nevertheless, off I went in the early morning of the following day, having decided on the rail to Inverness and hoping to find a coach or bus thereafter. Grandfather said he would try to contact Mr Benson to let him know that his files and notes were being retrieved. He phoned his daughter Alicia and she said she would let Mr Benson know, saying she could contact him.

I took my laptop with me on the train and was able to work away at my schoolwork online and get it all done. The internet connection on the train was surprisingly good. In general, though, I was really missing school—feeling the lack of formal lessons, missing the give-and-take with the teachers in the classroom, and missing the camaraderie of the other boys. I visited the buffet car twice, but the food was more a snack than a meal.

I was glad to arrive at Inverness Station and find the bus station a short walk away. The Stagecoach drivers were helpful and they discussed putting me on a bus that was going quite shortly in the direction of Grantown on Spey, but it was not going to be as close to my destination as I had hoped. I settled for the 34X bus toward Carrbridge. I asked the coach driver to let me off as near as possible to her village and asked him if he had any ideas on what I could do to complete the journey.

'Are there any local buses, do you think?'

'I think you will have to try and hitch a lift,' the coach driver said, showing me with a jerk of his thumb what I should do. 'Good luck!' he said when he set me down at a junction and pointed out the road and directions.

I got a lift for part of the way quite quickly—two women, one a district nurse, the other a schoolteacher, finishing work for the day and on their way home. But they were not willing to go any further out of their way at all to help me on my journey. They set me down where they normally turned off and pointed out that I had a good way further to go. I debated whether I should offer them money to take me further, but decided against it, hoping for another hitch—a decision I regretted later as nothing stopped for me. I trudged on. There was little traffic in this remote part, and few cars came whizzing by. None stopped or even slowed down. I plodded on. Dusk was falling. I was beginning to feel the cold.

Then, I got one last lift—a doctor on his rounds. Looking at my weary face and hearing that I had come all the way from London, he took me right to the door. He said he knew Mary Benson quite well and asked why I was coming to see her. I explained that her brother was my Housemaster at school and I was picking up her brother's teaching folders that he had left behind.

'How are you going to get back to London?' he asked.

'Well, she knows I am coming, and I assume she will have a meal for me and put me up for the night, and I can make my way home tomorrow.'

The doctor looked pensive. 'If you have a problem, ask her to phone me, Dr Hendricks, and I will come and pick you up,' he said. And with that, he drove off to continue his rounds.

I stood outside the house, which was shrouded in darkness. It stood on its own in an untended garden that looked a bit of a wilderness. There was no sign of life, no lights at the windows. She should have a porch light, I thought. I could hear no sound from the bell at the front door when I pressed it, so I knocked loudly as well. Then I called her name.

'Miss Benson! Miss Benson! I've come to pick up your brother's schoolwork folders!'

She came to the door and peered out at me. I repeated what I had said.

'I'll fetch them,' she said and went to bring a heavy stack of papers and folders, trying to thrust them at me. She looked at me a bit absently, I thought.

'I need to come in,' I said. 'I'll put them in my backpack.'

'Of course,' she said.

She consented to let me in, and I came through the hall and into her front room. Then I had a chance to look at her and the room. Like her brother, she was quite young—mid-thirties, I thought, perhaps a bit older than her brother—but I could see the family likeness. Whereas my Housemaster, Mr Benson, had a look of resolute determination and strength about him—anyone who could lead a House full of schoolboys needed that—his sister looked a bit vague and unfocused, as though her mind was elsewhere and she was thinking of something else. She had a pleasant face, pale blue eyes that didn't meet my gaze directly, no make-up, and wispy, out-of-control hair.

I stowed the Housemaster's work files into one section of my backpack. She stood and watched me. I looked around the room and saw at once that she was an artist. Whereas Alicia had any painting gear stacked meticulously away in a corner of her tidy flat, Miss Benson was using the whole room as a studio with an easel, a stool, and a small table—and why not, I thought, it was her house to do what she wanted in. I could understand, though, why Mr Benson had felt he could not bring four boys to stay there at half-term. It was a large room, and there was also a sofa and a table and chairs—a real living room—but it was clearly also her workspace.

I realised that I must say what I needed to say directly.

'Miss Benson, I have come all the way from London to fetch these. I left very early this morning. I hoped you would give me something to eat when I arrived, and you need to put me up until morning. I can't just turn around and start back to London.'

'I suppose not,' she said. 'What would you like to eat?'

'What are you having?' I asked.

'Let's look and see what we've got,' she said.

She hadn't taken offence that I had spoken so directly. She was obviously happy with plain-speaking. I put my backpack down and we went together into the kitchen, which I was relieved to see was quite organised. On the windowsill, she was growing herbs in brown earthenware pots. I spotted at once a tall, heavy glass jar of spaghetti.

'Spaghetti for two,' I said. 'Your brother made a splendid one for all of us on the first night in Tomintoul—spaghetti bolognese.'

'I taught him to cook,' she said. 'It's one of the things we had to be good at when we were younger and had to fend for ourselves. I don't always bother too much when I'm on my own.'

We opened the door of the refrigerator and found meatballs, tomatoes, and some round, earthy mushrooms. I was most impressed with the way she set about making the meal. Once the spaghetti was boiling away in a large salted saucepan of water, she had the mushrooms washed, sliced, and sweating in a pan in butter, the meatballs mashed up and lightly fried, the tomatoes skinned in boiling water, roughly chopped, and added. She reached across to the windowsill, snipped away at her herbs, and in went a small handful, all mixed up and stirred with a wooden spoon. She brought down two large, beautiful bowls and stood them ready to receive the food when it was cooked.

'What beautiful bowls,' I said. 'I've never seen anything like them in my life. Where do they come from?'

She was clearly pleased. 'I made them myself,' she said.

She gave me a small grater to add a little parmesan to the surface when we were ready to dish up.

The doorbell rang.

'Who on earth can that be?' she said.

'Shall I go?' I asked.

She nodded. To my amazement, the man who had given me a lift stood there—Dr Hendricks.

'It's Dr Hendricks,' I said. 'He gave me a lift when I was hitch-hiking the last leg to your house.'

'Ask him in,' said Miss Benson, reaching down for a third of her beautiful bowls for him. 'There's plenty of food for three. You never know with doctors whether they're going to be free to come, but get him to lay the table!'

'Marvellous smell of cooking,' he said.

The doctor cleared a space on her working table and set out utensils for the three of us. He switched on two bars of her small electric fire.

She brought in a large wooden bowl of salad—lettuce, spring onions, and tomatoes—that she had tossed together and plonked into the centre of the table. She shook a small glass carafe of her homemade vinaigrette and drizzled some on, then brought in the three bowls of steaming hot food and another three smaller bowls for the salad. It was my job to grate the parmesan onto the spaghetti in each bowl, apparently.

Dr Hendricks went to the kitchen and brought back three large, coarse white napkins, which he insisted we tucked into our collars at the neck.

'Essential when eating spaghetti!' he said.

He seemed quite at home in Mary Benson's house and opened a bottle of red wine that he had brought along. We each had a glass of cold tap water and an additional glass for the red wine, which the doctor had opened. They gave me a small amount. I was not really used to it, I told them, but it did go right to the right spot, I agreed.

We all three tucked in. The food was delicious. It did occur to me that she had made quite a lot of food and wondered whether Dr Hendricks had been expected all along.

Miss Benson switched off the bars on the electric fire.

'The room's quite warm now, we don't need that on. Spike looks as though he's falling asleep.'

'I am,' I said, and moved over to the sofa and sat down. I was terribly tired by then.

'I am quite happy on this couch,' I said. 'I shall need to get off in the morning. All I need now is just a blanket.' They laughed, and a thick rug was thrown over me and a cushion placed under my head. I lay down.

'Oh dear,' I said, half sitting up suddenly. 'I'm very good at washing up. Can I do that first?'

They protested that there was almost nothing to do, and I lay back, shut my eyes, and drifted off, hearing them talking away in the background as I let the tiredness from the journey slowly seep away. I slept, falling into a deep slumber after my long, stressful day, while Miss Benson and Dr Hendricks finished the wine and talked softly together. I thought they later took their coffee outside to sit in the moonlight.

Chapter 24

Studio and Pottery

I was wakened with a cup of strong tea in the morning. Dr Hendricks had gone to do his ward round and attend the local cottage hospital, as well as his general practitioner's morning clinic, but had said he might be back later, if he was free, and would give me a lift to a bus stop where the coach stopped that would take me on to the railway station.

'I should just like to draw you,' said Miss Benson, and told me where and how to sit. There was nothing for it but to sit as requested and submit to being drawn.

'This is just a preliminary charcoal sketch,' she said. 'I shall need to spend more time to do it in pencil and again to paint it and get the colours right.'

The washing up had been done by unseen hands last night. I had a small breakfast—toast and marmalade and more tea.

'Before you go, would you like to see where I make my bowls and do my pottery and clay work?' she asked, and led me out to a shed outside the back door. She lifted the latch and we went into her workshop.

The turning wheel, pins, and foot-pedal motor were all familiar to me from the Art Department at Ranford School, and I admired her compact set-up in the shed. I sat on the stool and imagined myself throwing a pot and shaping the clay. Under her work table was a bucket, damp with clay, and three further buckets stood to the side.

'It's marvellous,' I said.

Shelves on the wall held plates and bowls and mugs—some drying out and waiting to be fired, some waiting for painting before glazing—and on a wider shelf below, her instruments were neatly stacked: fettling knives, cut-off wires, callipers, wooden ribs, and potters' needles and brushes. She tidied around, gathering up her chamois scraps, and deposited them by the sponges that lay on a good square sink. She wiped her hands on a cloth.

'Where's your kiln?' I asked.

'Round the back in a bit of a lean-to. I don't want to gas myself—it's well ventilated out there.'

She reached up and handed me down a mug.

'You can have this one,' she said. 'It's the same colour and pattern as the bowls we ate from last night and that you admired. As you can see, it's not perfect—I got it a bit lopsided.'

It looked fine to me, and I thanked her.

Dr Hendricks looked in.

'I thought I'd find you here,' he said. 'I've got a few moments and can run Spike to the bus stop where he can catch the coach.' Then he added, 'That sketch of him is very good—it could go in your next exhibition.'

'It's just charcoal. I can do it again in pencil, and again as a portrait, but I will need to see him again to get the colours right.'

'We must go,' said Dr Hendricks, and added, 'Mary has no sense of time.'

'I think she's just inspirational,' I said. 'Miss Benson, I'm so glad to have met you at last and seen your house. And thank you for supper. And thank you for arranging for us to stay in the cottage in Tomintoul.'

'Oh, this is one of the boys who took all the trout from the streams in Tomintoul!'

I hoped Dr Hendricks was joking.

I shook hands solemnly with Miss Benson, stowed the mug carefully into my backpack, and checked carefully that I had all the Housemaster's files. Then I was off to meet up with the coach at the bus stop. Dr Hendricks left me at Carrbridge—just dropped me off with a cheery wave, didn't stop for thanks, and drove away back to his work.

There were not many buses during the day—perhaps only three—and to my great relief, the bus duly arrived at 13:22, the 34X, and would take about an hour to get to Inverness. The bus stopped a dozen times or so before arriving at the bus station in Inverness, and I had just under half an hour to get myself to the railway station and be organised.

The London train, I found, was due to leave at 14:50—ten to three—and I seemed to have some possible changes to look out for. I would arrive in London in the middle of the night, at quarter past one in the morning—1:13 am, if all went well—which concerned me a bit.

To pass the time while I checked the times and changes and waited for the train to arrive, I looked to see what the alternatives had been. The best I could see would have been to take the night sleeper leaving Inverness at 20:45—quarter to nine in the evening— and arriving at Euston rather than King's Cross at 07:49 am, quarter to eight the next morning. That sounded a much better bet. Either way, it seemed to be a nine or ten hour train journey.

I reflected that if I had had some way of getting from Miss Benson's house to Inverness Station yesterday evening, I could have got the train back to London the same day. Perhaps that was what Miss Benson thought I would do and why she had not planned to give me a meal and somewhere to stay for the night. Who knew, I thought.

Quite what time I would arrive now in London, I was not sure— it looked like one in the morning—and what it would be like at one in the morning at King's Cross, I had no idea. How I was going to get the teaching notes back to my Housemaster, I was also unsure. But I had done my best with fetching them.

At least, I reflected, I had met my Housemaster's sister—whom I had been so curious to meet—and had seen the house where she lived. And I felt it was entirely understandable that it would have been impossible for a group of her brother's boys from school to stay: her thoughts were all directed onto her creative work.

Ten hours on the train passed in a blur. The ticket collector was helpful with the changes, and I mostly dozed throughout the journey. Near the end, I asked somewhat tentatively what Kings Cross would be like at one in the morning, concerned whether it would be deserted. I was assured that it was quite lively—just the same at night as in the day, or even more so.

At last, the announcement was made over the tannoy: we were approaching London Kings Cross and passengers were reminded to take their bags with them. I shouldered my backpack and checked carefully which side the platform was on. I was ready to face the final stretch of my eventful few days.

I stepped down from the train and began the long, long walk along the platform towards the exit. And there, in the far distance, on the other side of the barrier—waiting for me—stood my Housemaster, Mr Benson, and Alicia. Relief swept over me.

To my tired brain, it seemed a complete coincidence. Then I wondered: were the folders and work notes so important that Mr

Benson had come to collect them immediately? Finally, my weary mind reached the more sensible conclusion that Miss Mary Benson had a better sense of time than Dr Hendricks gave her credit for. Either she—or perhaps Dr Hendricks himself—had phoned and passed on the message to Grandfather that I was on my way back, carrying the papers for my Housemaster, and had given the train's arrival time at Kings Cross. So they had come to meet me.

I voiced all these thoughts to myself, one after the other, in a mind muddled with tiredness.

'What a coincidence!' I said, as I reached the barrier.

We all three laughed. Mr Benson and Alicia placed themselves one on either side of me and walked me out of the station and into a taxi.

'Is Grandfather alright?' I asked with a sudden pang of worry.

'Very much so,' said Alicia, 'though why he thought it appropriate to let you go on such a marathon journey, I can't imagine.'

'How come you forgot your folders and notes when you left?' I asked Mr Benson.

'In my defence, I didn't forget them. I think my sister moved them from where I had put them. But I'm not blaming her—I should have checked.'

'Can I give them to you now?'

'I think we'll get you back to Maida Vale first, let Grandfather know you're back, and get you something to eat and drink. But thank you very much indeed for collecting them. Really—thank you.'

'At least I've met your sister and seen where she lives. I was very curious to. She's an extraordinary person. But the house is miles from anywhere,' I said.

Mr Benson laughed again. 'It is a bit remote. It's not so bad if you've got a car. Or a motorbike.'

I brought out the mug from my backpack. 'She gave me this. She makes lovely pottery. She showed me where she does her potting. But mostly, she paints.'

Alicia handled the mug with the hands of an artist.

'It is lovely,' she said. 'The colours.'

'We ate from bowls she'd made like this. They're beautiful. We cooked spaghetti bol—Dr Hendricks joined us—and I must say it was exceedingly good. I told her about your spaghetti bolognaise that you made for us all on the first night at Tomintoul, and she said that she'd taught you to cook that.'

'It's quite true,' said Mr Benson. 'We had to fend for ourselves for some years on our own, and she was a very supportive big sister to me. I was away at school at first, and she was at college doing her training. We both came back home at intervals, then I left again for university and college, and now for work—so she was very much on her own. But she was always there for me when I needed her. I owe her a lot. And she is very, very talented.'

'We're getting a debriefing,' Alicia said. 'Who is Dr Hendricks?'

'He was my second hitch-hike,' I said. 'First I had a nurse and a schoolteacher on their way home from work, and then Dr Hendricks, who took me all the way as he knows Mary Benson. Then he turned up for supper with a bottle of wine.'

'Did they give you wine?' both Alicia and Mr Benson asked together.

'They gave me a bit,' I said. 'It wasn't much for me.'

***

We sat for a short time while I had my hot chocolate and biscuits, and while I unburdened myself further about my experiences. I handed over the trophy files and papers.

'I hope they're all there,' I said.

'I'm sure they will be.'

'I've probably got some more online work from school waiting for me,' I added. 'I did some on the train on the way up, but I didn't manage any on the way back. I might just take a look.'

'I think you should take a book and go to bed,' Mr Benson said. 'You'll probably unwind and fall asleep.'

'We'll see ourselves out. Lock up for Grandfather. He went back to sleep at once when we told him you were back. He muttered at us

186

that Mrs Clarke had said you were very resourceful and not to worry.'

'Did he say that? Did she say that? That I was very resourceful? *Resourceful!* I like that!'

I took a book and went to bed, placing my new mug on the bedside table.

Chapter 25

Hard Times the Housemaster and Alicia

Rob Benson and Alicia Kingswell left Spike, locking up for his grandfather before he got off to bed, and they set off for Little Venice together. They began walking side by side. As they crossed over the first road, she tucked her hand into his arm. It was dark and late, and they continued walking closely in harmony, their arms linked.

As they approached Little Venice, he placed his arm across her shoulders.

'I'll need to leave first thing tomorrow morning, Alicia. I'm keen to get down to Ranford, to the school now. I've got all my papers and notes, and I must get down to preparing lessons for streaming to the boys. The Headmaster will expect me to be ready to put in some work.'

'Is that it then?' she said. 'I hoped it was something more than a brief interlude.'

'It's been wonderful,' he said. 'Wonderful to meet you. In different circumstances, things might have moved on. But these are strange times. The country is going into lockdown with the spread of this virus. And it's not like the beginning of the World Wars, when people made hasty liaisons as a soldier was leaving for the battlefront, or a pilot to his airfield, grasping for happiness, not knowing when—or whether—they would come back. We live in the here and now, and I have work to do for the school. We've come across each other because of our very different connections with Spike. As his Housemaster, I feel a strong duty of responsibility to him—and indeed to all the boys in my House at school—but particularly I feel it for Spike because of his vulnerable situation. And in fact, you must know that because of our very different connections with him, I can't see any possibility for you and me to be more than we are now.'

She laughed. 'We're like two concerned parents!' she said.

'Exactly!' He laughed too, then went on:

'I know what I have to do now—get on with my teaching work. I also know what *you* should do. With the world coming to a halt in a way, and with the strange situation you've been put in—seize your chance now, Alicia. Return to academic study. Go for that degree you should have done. Three or four years on, life will have changed—and you must be ready for it. Promise me you'll give it a go.'

'I'll look into it, Rob. I just want to say—it has been wonderful meeting you. It's made making that connection with Spike so much more possible. Easier.'

'He is an unusual boy, isn't he? So resilient.'

'*Resourceful!* He's funny. So proud the Headmaster's wife, Mrs Clarke, called him resourceful.'

'She's a powerful lady, Mrs Clarke. All of us schoolmasters are wary of her. In awe of her.'

They were silent for a while.

'We both hold Spike very dear in our hearts—he's such a remarkable boy.'

'*Resourceful!*'

'Don't mock! But I feel very strongly that you should go back to formal education and make up for what you missed out on.'

'I went to Art College for three years.'

'You did. I acknowledge that. But you chose Art College rather than university because it was easier to get into without the support of school. Alicia, if you could see the passion which my sister puts into her art work—her painting, her drawing—charcoal and pencil and paints. Her pottery. Exhibiting. She has given up a lot to pursue that. I don't know who this Dr Hendricks is—but if he's a man friend or a lover, I for one will be delighted. I must have been a bit blind not to see how fed up she was with having her brother foisted on her as a live-in lodger if she has a boyfriend in the vicinity. I don't think you feel that same passion for art.

'I'm going to make a suggestion. That you think over what you would like to do—and go to university for four years and do it. We will still have a connection with each other. In four years' time, Spike will be leaving school.

'Alicia, I think the uncertainty of this virus epidemic has caused us all to react as though we were on the brink of going to war. People reacted like this, I believe, before the nation embarked on each of the two World Wars—accelerating relationships, grasping at opportunities, before it was all too late.

'Let's take it leisurely and get on with the work we have before us.'

'We'll talk again tomorrow when we've had a good night's sleep,' Alicia said. 'Then I have to decide what I want to study—and what courses are possible in epidemic time.'

'True.'

Chapter 26

Alicia Takes Stock

Once my Housemaster had departed for Ranford School to help the Head continue delivering the online lessons, I saw Alicia begin to take stock of her situation.

I found her sitting at a table in Grandfather's study, going through all her old school reports.

'I am looking to see what I could do if I went back to studying. Mr Benson thinks I should go back to college and work seriously. I wondered about Philosophy. The best bet seems to be Criminal Psychology. Maybe it's best to study Law first and move across into criminal psychology. Maybe I can do that through the Open University.'

She said she had gone through her Art equipment in her flat and put it straight. It had always looked very orderly and tidy — very much so, I thought, compared with Mary Benson's.

'I have a commission waiting to be done, to illustrate a children's storybook,' she said. 'I have to draw a loveable beagle on every page. I should have got round to it.'

She had collected a sheaf of downloaded pictures of beagles and cut-outs from newspapers and magazines to provide inspiration. She said she had let the commissioning agent know that she had free time to get on with it now and would move ahead with it. She had gathered the script she'd been sent and a supply of paper into a folder and put them with her small portable Cotman travel bag of watercolours, soft pencils, palette and sketchpad.

'I'm getting organised,' she said.

Mrs Robinson popped her head round the door to ask if Alicia would be staying for lunch, which she accepted.

Mrs Robinson, when shown the photographs from the little metal box, was extremely interested to see the pictures. Like Grandfather, she had never met Pat and Tony and was fascinated to see the photos of them, the series from my childhood, and the snap of Alicia and my father taken fifteen years ago. She probably took more interest in the photos than anyone, apart from myself.

'My old school reports,' Alicia said, as she was reading them now, 'are an eye-opener. I must have seen them briefly at the time. I probably scan-read them to see if any of the teachers had written anything vengeful about me,' she said. 'I don't think either of my parents ever bothered much to look at my reports properly. My school was academically excellent, but a rather stiflingly conventional all-girls' school, and it's clear to me, reading these reports now, that the schoolteachers had been assiduous in assessing the girls' progress and potentials, painstakingly recording their opinions of our abilities and future potential. I was never really aware of that.'

She was jotting down the odd phrase on a bit of paper. 'I'm impressed with how good they thought I was!' she told me.

She came finally to the last report before she had had to leave the school. She thought they would have been condemnatory, but it was not so at all. There was regret at wasted potential but nothing worse. She came at last to her form teacher's last word on her. She read it out.

'Alicia has a fine analytical brain that would be put to good use in philosophy or law and she should consider pursuing that option, perhaps in psychology and criminal law, rather than taking a degree in general humanities.' Well, there it was in black and white. Why had I not read that before?' she asked. 'I went to Art School because I could get in there without needing the school's support and I did enjoy my time there and did well at it. I am a competent artist rather than an inspired one. It has never occurred to me until now that I could go back and study again.'

She switched on Grandfather's computer and started to look up where she could study psychology and criminal law, starting in September of the next academic year, including the Open University. It was interesting for me to observe how she went about investigating where the courses were.

We sat over lunch in the kitchen. Alicia told us — Grandfather and me — how she had been looking at her options on the computer and outlined her plans for the future.

'I think I might let my flat for three to six months or longer, which would give me some income, and go to study and take just a room wherever I can go to do the course.'

She said, 'Now you've told me all about Mary Benson's art and pottery set-up, Spike, I'm very tempted to go and look at it myself. She's obviously much better than I am, in a different class, but if I do I'll not go on the Night Sleeper or whatever it is that you describe, or even the train. I would take the cheapest bus and coach there is.'

'I think the Night Sleeper sounds great fun,' I said. 'I would definitely choose that another time.'

'But much more expensive,' she said.

Grandfather said, 'You might have a fairy godmother who would treat you.'

I got the message at once. Or a fairy father, did he mean? Grandfather was wonderful.

Grandfather said, 'If you let your flat and go on your travels or become a student somewhere else, please write to *Spike and me*, or to *me and Spike*, whichever you prefer, and let us both know all that you are getting up to. We'll look out for your letters and news, won't we, Spike?'

'We will.'

***

Mrs Robinson looked in on us before she left.

'I think, Spike, my nephew will be coming out of Feltham shortly, and he's going to need his bicycle back. Do you want to ride it over to the Estate?'

'I will. I'll do it this afternoon. It was very kind of him to lend it to me.'

'Well, he probably doesn't know he lent it until we tell him. You can walk back with me later this afternoon if you want.'

Chapter 27

Disaster

I set off with Mrs Robinson to the Estate, me wheeling the bike. It was an effort to get the bike and both of us into the lift, but the bike had to go up and be somewhere safe, or it would be stolen. We reached the 27th floor and extracted the bike from the lift, wheeling it along the balcony passageway.

There, sitting on the ground, knees to chest, leaning against Mrs Robinson's door, was a youth — scruffy in the modern manner: sneakers, tracksuit bottoms at half-mast, biker's jacket.

'Hello, Auntie,' he said.

'Darren, this is Spike. I got Spike to take care of your bike while you were in. Otherwise, it might have gone missing.'

'Thanks, mate,' said Darren.

'It was a great help, your bike,' I said. 'I had a job to do off the Gray's Inn Road, and it was a bit dicey. I could have done with you to watch my back. My father asked me to collect something for him.'

'His father's in the Scrubs,' offered Mrs Robinson, 'but likely there'll be no more prison visits with this virus.'

Darren whistled. He was clearly impressed. 'Scrubs! Wow! You need more help in the future — you ask me,' he said.

'I wouldn't mind taking a second look at the place sometime. See if it's changed,' I said.

'We'll go now,' said Darren.

'It's a tidy step over there. We'd need a second bike.'

'No way. You sit on the saddle and I'll pedal.'

'Now don't you go getting into any more trouble, Darren, my lad. You've only just got out of the last lot.'

'I ain't done nuffin,' said Darren.

And we set off, manoeuvring the bicycle down the lift again, and cycling away between the tower blocks, taking a circuitous route to the Gray's Inn Road, keeping off the main roads so that we wouldn't be spotted and stopped in our irregular mode of travel — with Darren doing all the work, half-sitting on the cross-bar, standing on the pedals, his feet working away, and me sitting on the saddle with my legs dangling either side.

We reached the narrow carriage entrance on the Gray's Inn Road and got off the bike, walking it down the cobbled cul-de-sac behind the houses, wheeling it between us.

'Ace!' Darren approved of the funny little street. 'Which one's your building?'

'Right at the end,' I said. 'At the far end, there's a low wall and a small park on the other side. I put the bike over the wall and lay it on its side, then when I was ready to make a getaway, I vaulted over the wall, grabbed the bike and pedalled away.'

'Nice one,' said Darren. 'Which is the house?'

'The end one, or it was. What's happened to it?'

The end house looked as though a bomb had hit it. The far end wall of number 4 was beginning to crumble into the rubble that had always lain alongside it. The lobby seemed to have been boarded up, but the planks nailed across the entrance were gaping apart, as though someone still needed access and had wrenched them open to come and go.

'Annie lived in this one, the ground floor room,' I pointed out. 'She was a little old lady, bent in two, but talkative. I never saw anyone on the next floor. Then Eric was above — a big, tough guy. He came and went. Then Alf, who hands out the newspapers of an evening at the steps down to the tube, was on the top floor, and he hung his key in the broom cupboard on that top floor whenever he went out. That was the room I had to go into and collect something for my father — up the stairs, collect the key, go in, and run my hands in the gap between the top of the door and the gable to find a little box.'

'Well, you done it.'

'When I came down with it, I had to hide beneath the stairs until the Heavies had gone. There was a sink and a toilet that they all used at the back under the stairs. Then I went over the wall there and cycled away.'

'What's the Heavies like?'

'Threatening.'

'You did OK!'

'There's more. I'd made sure Alf had gone to his work where he handed the newspapers out every evening at the mouth of the tube station, and when I climbed the stairs, I took the key from the cubby-hole cupboard and opened his door. It was pretty dark inside, and I thought there was no one there, but then I nearly jumped out of my skin — because there was something sitting there. A spectre, sitting on the bed, sitting cross-legged. A poor little child with staring eyes. It didn't move. It didn't say anything. Just stared.'

Like the spectre, Darren was speechless.

'But Darren, don't you see? Maybe she's still there!'

Darren was made of sterner stuff. 'Well, we'll go and see.' And he pulled the boards blocking the entrance to the lobby a little further apart with his bare hands and hopped through the gap. I took a little time to follow.

'Where've you been?' said Darren.

'I've moved the bike out of sight round the side.'

'Nice one,' said Darren. It was one of his favourite sayings.

The door to Room A on the ground floor stood agape. There was no sign of Annie.

'No sign of Annie,' I said.

'She's probably been carted away to an Old Peoples' Home.'

Room B remained firmly shut. 'I never saw it open.'

Up, up we went, up further stairs. We opened the door to Room C. Eric, the tough guy, had decamped and left, leaving behind a collection of vests and singlets and a pair of braces, strewn across an unmade bed. There was no sign of his recent presence.

As we made our way up the last set of stairs, the whole staircase shuddered and felt unstable. I went first and turned, pointing out for Darren to look on the right-hand side:

'Look, there used to be a cubby-hole here — right there on the right-hand side. This is where the key to Room D was hung, but it's totally missing. The broom cupboard just seems to have fallen away, leaving a thin jagged wall.' I touched the plaster — maybe gave it a little shove to see where it had gone to — and with that, there was an enormous heave, and the stairway beneath our very feet began slowly to crumble.

Down and down and down we went — with a crack and a bang — everything giving way and collapsing slowly, subsiding, until we both, Darren and I, were slowly carried earthward, vertically down three flights together with plasterboard and wood, a few tiles, the staircase, and a stash of rubble. A slow crumbling descent until we reached the ground, tumbling and slowly falling, and finally we were buried under a cloud of dust, lying on fallen masonry and the rotten wood of the staircase.

There we lay at first. Lay still. Breathing dust. Our legs and bodies were trapped under rubble. Stunned. No idea where we were. We could see nothing through the clouds of white plaster dust. Slowly, over the next many minutes—it felt like half an hour or so— the dust began to settle and clear away.

'Darren?' I called.

'I'm here!' he said. 'Say, Spike, lucky you moved the bike out the way!' And he laughed.

With that touch of humour in the midst of disaster, I knew that I had found a stalwart companion, a good friend, and I thought we were going to be all right.

'What happened to the little staring child sitting cross-legged?' I asked.

'You're not going to believe this,' said Darren, 'but she's here, sitting next to me. We seem to have rescued her.'

It was my turn to try for humour: 'Lucky we came to rescue her then.' It fell a bit flat.

'I am slowly going to extricate myself,' I said. 'Bit by bit, move this stuff off me.'

'You do talk posh sometimes. But when you've finished extricating yourself, have a go at digging me out.'

'I will.'

Without pulling more rubble onto us, I did manage to get myself clear—first sit, then stand—and went over and lifted stuff off Darren.

'Cor, that's a relief!' he said, and levered himself into the sitting position.

'What shall we do with the little lady?' asked Darren. 'She doesn't seem to be hurt. What say we take her round to the steps by the tube station and give her to the bloke that hands out the newspapers? Alf, wasn't it?'

'I think we probably need an ambulance. Maybe the police.'

'The polis?' I could see at once that Darren was not keen.

'The polis?' he repeated. 'I don't think so.'

The situation was saved by a figure hastening down the cul-de-sac.

'It's Alf! Look, here comes Alf! Alf to the rescue, I should say!'

He did indeed rescue the situation. He scooped up the child, who hardly reacted. Alf spoke to me, whom he recognised.

'We've got somewhere to go at last. I'll take her off. Thank you for seeing to her. Social Services have got us a place to go to. Temporary, anyway. Looks like the whole building is coming down.'

'Before you go, Alf, what happened to the others? Annie? Eric?'

He answered tersely. 'Annie? Old People's Home, 34 Mile End Road. Should have gone there yonks ago. Near one of her daughters. But wanted to be on her own. Couldn't cope, really.' He paused. 'Eric—Eric can always find a place. Got a missus someplace. And another missus some-other-place-else. So this was a getaway for him.'

'And Room B? Always locked?'

'Always locked. That's right. That's where they stored the stuff.'

'Has it all gone now? The stuff?'

'I should expect so. They'll have collected it.'

I addressed Alf again. 'Alf, have you taken all the stuff you want from your place? It's all come down.'

'There's nothing I want that's there. I'll start again. I'll be in the Salvation Army refuge near Farringdon if you want me. To start with. But they've got Social Services involved and they're thinking of a flat in Peckham. We'll see.' And with that, cradling the unresponsive child, he went on his way.

'Shall we get home, Darren?'

'Have a look at the bike, Spike, if you will.'

I wheeled it round. It looked undamaged.

'It was a good move, shifting it out the way. But I won't be able to pedal it home. But I can sit on it if you can walk the bike home with me sitting on the saddle.'

'I'll try.'

I felt it was the least I could do, having led Darren into such a disaster. With much moaning and groaning, we somehow got Darren on to the bike and, leaning on me, we set off to walk our way home. It took a good time and, as we neared home, we held a debate as to where we should aim for—the Estate and Baer Tower or Hamilton Terrace and Maida Vale. Darren chose the Estate and his Auntie, Mrs Robinson.

'Just get me up to Auntie's,' he said. 'She'll see me right. If she needs to take me to the hospital for an X-ray or anything, she'll borrow a wheelchair and push me round there. We've done it before for one or another. You take the bike back with you. I won't be wanting to pedal it for a little while. But come and see me,' he said. 'I got something I want you to do for me.'

'Anything,' I said. 'I'm afraid I've led you into a pack of trouble.'

***

When we got to the Tower Block, Baer Tower, I propped the bike with Darren sitting on it against the wall and went ahead to bring Mrs Robinson down to help get Darren back off the bike, into the lift and along the corridor.

It wasn't going to be an easy conversation to have with Mrs Robinson.

I rang the chiming bell on her door. She looked through the spyhole and called, 'Who is it?'

'It's me, Spike. I've brought Darren back. We've had a bit of an accident. He's downstairs by the lift but I'll need your help to get him back up here.'

I half expected her to tell me to go away, but Mrs Robinson was made of sterner stuff—stalwart in the face of disaster, experienced in the face of emergencies—and down she came at once, propping her door open to receive the wounded soldier, as she called him. She took one look at both of us, covered with dust and grime, and expressed her disgust that we had only been gone a couple of hours and couldn't stay out of trouble. And off she went in a tirade of protest.

We got Darren off the bike and managed to sit him on the floor of the lift, then up we went to the 27th floor. Darren humped himself out of the lift and crawled over to sit on a rug and doormat that Mrs Robinson produced and had laid on the ground. He sat there nursing his injured knee and ankles.

Mrs Robinson and I tugged and dragged the rug bearing her injured nephew along the corridor and into her flat.

Mrs Robinson then made herself very clear. 'I will manage both bath and bandages for Darren and anything else needed, and you, Spike, can take yourself off back to your grandfather and get yourself cleaned up.'

'Yes, Mrs Robinson, I'm very sorry, Mrs Robinson,' was all I could manage.

Darren gave me a wink and said, 'See you later, Spike. Take care of my bike.'

I managed to bypass seeing Grandfather as I wheeled the bike back into the hall.

'I see you've still got the bike,' Grandfather called.

'Yes, and I'm a bit grubby. I'll just take a bath and be right down for supper.' When I came down, I was in my pyjamas and dressing gown and ready for an early night once we had eaten. As far as I could see or feel, I had not sustained any injuries myself. While I hoped it might be the same for Darren, I feared it might not be.

Chapter 28
Exclusion

Next morning, there was no sign of Mrs Robinson. I got my schoolwork done online as swiftly as possible and set off at once on foot to see how Darren was doing. I found him sitting up on the sofa-bed—the settee that could be moved down from sofa to couch to bed—clean and washed, lying propped up against cushions with his feet up and covered with a blanket.

'Am I pleased to see you?' said Darren. 'I got a right wigging from Auntie. She seems to think I led you astray when we both know it's the other way round.'

'I am sorry, Darren. Are you much hurt?'

Darren pulled aside the blanket to show impressive bruises on his legs and a swollen ankle.

'I don't think anything's broken actually,' he said. 'The Probation's been up to see me and brought my gear from Feltham. They're quite relieved to see I can't get up to any more mischief at the moment—he made a joke about it. He'll look in again. He and Auntie understand each other. He brought my gear. He's a good bloke. Sit on the edge of the sofa, Spike, will you? He wants you to read to me.'

'To read to you?'

'Yeah!'

'Well, of course I will if that's what you want. What shall I read?'

Darren bent down and retrieved a pack of books and exercise books and a couple of pencils from under the sofa. 'I made a start in Feltham and he said I was doing quite well but I need to keep it up.'

I took the books and thumbed through them, and saw at once what they were: *You Can Read. A Teaching Guide. Teach an Adult to Read.* And some exercise books in which Darren had made a start.

'What fun,' I said. 'Do you want to do some now? We'll do some every day. About an hour? Or maybe twice a day. We'll romp through these.'

'I think I'll take a couple of paracetamol if you give me two and a glass of water—two of those pills from the mantelpiece. My leg throbs, and then I'll show you what I've done so far. We'll start proper tomorrow. He said do the exercise in the morning and a practice read in the afternoon, going over what we've done in the morning. You owe me, bruv!'

***

It was like nothing I had ever done before, and I planned to set about it with enthusiasm. I liked Darren—his tough, have-a-go-at-anything spirit. And I felt badly that I had been the cause of his being laid up with bruises and pain. I thought it would be an interesting, even fascinating, project. It would provide us with something to do that would occupy us both while school remained closed, at any rate until September, when I hoped lockdown would be finished, schools would open up again, and I would be able to go right back into school.

My own work and sessions reading with Darren would certainly help pass the time until then. By September, I expected Darren would be able to read well, and we could progress to boys' stories— *Alex Ryder*, paperbacks of *James Bond*, and suchlike.

Actually, I knew nothing whatsoever about how people learned to read or failed to do so, and was more optimistic than the situation warranted, but I was prepared to give it a go.

Grandfather, however, once I told him about it, was bowled over. He regarded the whole enterprise with enormous enthusiasm. It was a heaven-sent opportunity for him. It was just up his street— the access to education and the change it meant to the individual. At once, he put in an order which came by post for a whole series of large-format, large-print paperback books intended for school teachers to take their children through the various stages of primary school and with SATs. And equally, it was for parents to help their children learn. This was Grandfather's chance to see and do in practice what he wrote about in theory.

First, Grandfather said he needed to assess the particular deficiencies and problems with the skills—or lack of them—of his housekeeper's nephew, to identify where the gaps were, analyse what was the difficulty in his ability to read, and then determine how best to put them right.

As sometimes happens, apparently, some people with problems in one direction are possessed with special gifts in another. And, as it happened, this turned out to be quite marked in Darren's case— which made him a particularly interesting and important subject for Grandfather to study.

For all Grandfather's erudition and learning, for all his writings, his studies had all been theoretical. He had never had a live problem to study before. For him, Darren was the chance of a lifetime.

However, Darren was a boy, almost a young man, a person—not just a convenient case for study. Presented with these test papers and investigations, Darren showed a marked reluctance to the intrusion of being examined.

It was going to take all my diplomatic skills to persuade Darren to be willing to take any other tests. We just got down to his reading practice together because that was where he knew he needed help.

I took Grandfather's paperback learning books over, but Darren was really not interested in looking at them, and I had to put them to one side and just leave them with him. As I left, I casually suggested he might make a start on one, just to humour me—and out of boredom, laid up on the settee sofa in Mrs Robinson's flat, he did just that.

When I arrived the next morning, Darren thrust a sheaf of papers at me.

'I done those papers you wanted,' he said. 'I done the Maths. They was easy, and I like them. I'll do more if you got more.'

I looked at them. 'That's the whole lot!' I said. 'You've done the whole lot of the maths! In one evening. That's about five years of tests!'

'I couldn't sleep. My leg aches. They're easy, and I just carried on. It takes my mind off things. I made a start on the Reading ones and they're going to be useful, but I want to do those together with you.'

I couldn't wait to get the maths papers back to Grandfather but realised I should take it quietly, without fuss. We sat together, Darren and I, on Mrs Robinson's sofa-bed and continued to make slow progress on the reading practice. And it really was slow.

The test papers I carried back to Grandfather's study. The results were quite astonishing. Darren had raced through the mathematics and logical reasoning, making few mistakes. He had got through quite a substantial body of work. Where numbers were involved, he was confident and accurate.

Grandfather and I were both astonished how quick Darren's mind was as he raced through the maths problems. As it happened,

Grandfather had also ordered the next five years of test papers, really for himself in order to see the structure of the tests. He asked me to take the next batch of mathematics over to the Estate right away so that he could see how Darren's mind worked. This would take Darren up to and beyond his present age group for mathematics.

I took them over the next day and very casually laid them down—the next set of maths books—putting them to one side and said, 'If you can't sleep tonight, there's more of those maths here. I'm sorry your leg aches. You're marvellous at never complaining but it's not good to be in pain all the time. Now, let's get back down to the reading. Where would you like to start today? Let's read together. Alternate lines.'

***

Once the next set of maths results were received—equally well and speedily done—Grandfather could not be kept away from the project.

'Spike, I'd like to go over there and meet up with Darren and have a few words with him.'

'Grandfather, I don't think you can do that.' I paused to see how I could best put it to him. 'He's confined to lying with his leg up to give his injuries time to heal. It was my fault taking him to see that tenement building where I'd gone to get the metal box for my father and we had an accident there—we brought the whole side of the house down on top of us actually, or what remained of it. But he's holed up now with his bruises and strained knee and swollen ankle, and slowly healing,' I paused, 'but that's not even the reason you can't go and see him. He's lying on the sofa bed in Mrs Robinson's front room—well, it's really almost the only room in the flat and that's her home. It's bad enough me dropping in and out all the time. I try to be no trouble and I do keep Darren from boredom, but I don't think she'll want you invading her home. Well—I suppose you could ask her.'

'Oh dear! I don't think I want to hear the ins and outs of what you got up to with that wretched box of your father's. All for a handful of photographs. But I'll have a word with Mrs Robinson.'

I was right. When Grandfather spoke to Mrs Robinson, asking if he could come over and speak with her nephew, Mrs Robinson was very reluctant to have him visit her home. She had just the one living room in her flat and her settee was being occupied by her injured nephew, night and day. She explained that I, Spike, when I came, could perch on the sofa bed with Darren. There was room only for one other easy chair in the room—a chair on which she now had perforce to sit each evening. The last thing she wanted was to have the gentleman she 'did for' as housekeeper sitting in that chair and talking away to her nephew. Where was she meant to go? Where was she meant to put herself? Go and sit on the bed in her bedroom? In her own flat! No, she was not agreeable for him to come over. He had never asked before.

Grandfather realised he had not been diplomatic in the way that he had asked. He tried a different tack with her. He asked her casually, when she was busy in our kitchen with just the three of us there,

'What school did Darren go to?'

'No school,' she said tersely. 'No school, Mr Kingswell.'

'I mean before all the schools were closed down with this virus epidemic?'

'No school,' she repeated. 'Excluded.'

Grandfather was shocked. 'Excluded from which school?'

'Excluded from quite a few. Actually, excluded from every school he's been to.'

'How long has it been that he's been excluded?'

'On and off since starting secondary school. Age 11. On and off. Mostly off. Excluded means you're not in school. You're on the streets. And there's nothing to do. So then you get into trouble. Feltham recently. That wasn't pleasant for him, actually. But what can you do?'

Grandfather was learning more than he had expected. He didn't know what he could offer. But he did know that he wanted to include Darren's learning experiences both in his book and in a paper he was due to present once this virus shut-down was over.

When asked, I reported that Darren was making definite progress with his reading but it was slow—very slow—but there was some improvement. He was making some progress.

'I want to test his spatial awareness,' said Grandfather. 'If I give you some puzzles for him to solve, could you see if he will do them?'

I agreed and reported back, 'He quite likes them and has done them all, but not as much as the maths, which he really likes, if you have any more of those.'

The next step in mathematics was advanced maths—pure and applied, calculus, and statistics—and really needed a teacher to explain the initial steps. I appealed to Ranford School and Mr Benson in particular, who sent particulars of online programmes of advanced mathematics—but making it clear that they were for Mr Kingswell's interest in his studies and writings on education and society, and were way in advance of anything that Spike should be given. But the information gave Grandfather the link to access the next steps that were needed for Darren.

Grandfather located the online programme that he thought would do, showed it to me, and I took my own laptop over to Darren and showed him the ropes. At once, Darren was enthusiastic about it and really chuffed to be doing it on my laptop.

Darren's Probation Officer was a star and had located internet connection in the Tower Block. He was pleased and most impressed by the progress that Darren was making.

There was one snag. And it was more than a snag for me. It was not really practical for Darren in the Tower Block and me in Grandfather's house in Maida Vale to share a laptop computer. Once connected up, Darren was exceedingly reluctant to have that laptop taken off his knees. He became obsessively attached to his online mathematics. I appealed to Darren's Probation Officer, who said he would see what he could do, but clearly he was not going to be able to produce something out of the hat any time soon.

Fortunately for me, there had been a lull in the online streaming from my school. But the situation of the shared laptop could not be stalled forever. Meanwhile, I did have the bike—Darren's bike—and I could get up and about outside in spite of the increasing restrictions on lockdown that were being imposed all the time. No one bothered about a boy on a bike.

Chapter 29

Darren's Bike

Darren's bike was a joy to me. It opened up the whole world of London.

In spite of lockdown, I was able to make excellent use of that bike. I found that no one stopped a cyclist zooming round London, maybe assuming that I was delivering something. There were fewer cars on the road, much less traffic, fewer people around and about.

I remembered Alf's words about where the little old lady from 4A had been moved to, and looked up the route to 34 Mile End Road on my A-Z atlas. I cycled down to see Annie in the Old Peoples' Home.

I found her there in the living room, sitting in a communal space lined with upright easy chairs all arranged around the walls of the large reception room and all occupied by old ladies. One old gentleman sat there, but all the rest—*all* the rest—were ladies. I spotted Annie at once and took an empty chair beside her.

They were in the midst of a music-and-movement exercise, and most of the inhabitants, those who could do it, were waving their arms, shrugging their shoulders, flapping their hands, turning their heads to right and to left, waggling their feet and tapping their toes, and at the same time having a sing-a-long. I seemed to be accepted as some sort of volunteer and sat along with the others, taking part in the work-out. It was quite fun.

The volunteer pianist and therapist were enthusiastic and quite skilled at keeping it going, encouraging those who were able to join in and tolerant of those who were just observers. We finished with a communal clap to thank the pianist. The organiser began to pack up and leave after their session, and I was able to look around.

The ladies were all wearing identical small tortoiseshell hairbands, including Annie, that kept their brushed hair out of their eyes, and some had Alice bands also—all left behind by a previous inhabitant who had now departed, having no more use for any hairbands.

Annie offered to show me her room. It was pleasant and cheerful, looking out onto the small terrace and back garden—a distinct improvement on 4A Marchmont House in Little Great Middleton Street.

'I've got my own things here,' she said, pointing them out. There were few enough of them, nothing like Mrs Robinson's china ornaments, but she was proud of her possessions.

'I should have done this years ago,' she went on. 'Go into a home. I'm in clover here. I'm quite near my daughter but they've only visited me the once. You never did my Family Tree, did you?'

I was able to tell her that Alf was alright and was being looked after by the Salvation Army, and that he was hopeful that the Social Services were getting him a flat in Peckham.

'A flat in Peckham?' Annie sniffed at that. 'Chance would be a fine thing!' she said. She seemed to know nothing of the little cross-legged person, and when I mentioned it, she didn't seem to know what I was talking about.

There was no news from Eric, she said, but she had little doubt that he would be alright with one or other of his ladies.

'I must go now,' she said, meaning that I should go. 'You should be getting along, I don't want to miss my lunchtime.' And she took herself off, standing and walking much better than before—still bent but lively.

'Ta-ta! You can come again and visit me if you like!' she said with a wave of her hand.

***

The occasional short letter came from Alicia relating interesting accounts of what she was up to. She wrote jointly to me and Grandfather, usually 'Dear Dad and Spike', sometimes 'Dear Spike and Dad', and we shared the news. She was making good progress with providing the illustrations for the children's book, and she was hopeful that it would lead to further commissions for her artwork.

She was making a start with her new studies at the Open University. She was doing an introductory course, which seemed to be mandatory before you could sign on to a formal study programme. There was a choice of short courses. She had chosen one on her own family history and had commented wryly that she had thought hers would be unique and an interesting family history to do, but she had rapidly found out, she wrote, that her story was not as unusual and exceptional as she had imagined.

She had sub-let her flat in Little Venice at a very good rent, so she was not short of money. She had trekked up to visit the Benson house in the Highlands of Scotland, made friends with Mary Benson, and admired her paintings and pottery. She wrote that both Mary and Dr Hendricks had talked a great deal about me and of my visit, which had been quite a highlight for them both and, she thought, brought them together, apparently cementing their friendship.

I didn't agree with that. 'They seemed quite good friends already when I was there,' I commented, remembering Dr Hendricks switching on the two bars of the electric fire and fetching the table napkins, being ordered to lay the table, and saying that 'Mary' had no sense of time. Miss Benson later switched the fire off, saying the room was quite warm enough, and he was very complimentary about the charcoal sketch she did of me.

Grandfather continued to do his writing. Life went on. The improvement in Darren's reading abilities was slowly coming along. However, the problem of sharing the laptop loomed heavily over me, uncertain how I could get it back off him and reclaim it for myself. I would need it back for the start of term, and Darren was getting increasingly possessive about it. I didn't want to fall out with him, but I would need to take my laptop back.

As these things do, it suddenly resolved itself.

I was cycling along Little Venice and stopped to look at the communal noticeboard that the canal boat and barge people shared on a hoarding. Messages of all sorts were posted on it, and it formed a hub for the community of people who lived around. There, amongst the messages, I saw an advertisement:

FOR SALE

A laptop computer, good working order, surplus to requirements.

Buyer collects. Bargain at £120.

The Mary Lou.

I read it several times. Then I walked up and down along the line of the barges, looking to locate which of the many canal boats was the Mary Lou. It was a trim, well-kept boat.

One hundred and twenty pounds!

This is why one has money, I thought.

And the thought struck me forcibly.

I remembered Alicia's words as she surveyed the quantity of notes that lay beneath the photos: 'Life – if you have a little money behind you,' she said, 'Life is transformed – Money is enabling – Money gives you choices.'

And – I did have money.

And I didn't need to ask anyone.

And whether the money was actually mine or not, I would go ahead and use it.

Or use some of it.

Actually – it was only a very small part of it.

Chapter 30

The Canal Boat

I laid my plans. Back at home in Grandfather's house, I quietly went up to my room and sat on my bed. I was very happy to have a bedroom that was my ownroom. In my childhood, with Pat and Tony, I had naturally had my own bedroom, having no brothers or sisters. At school, of course, we were all in a dormitory; there were cubicles, but it was not the same as a room of one's own. Now, in Grandfather's house, his spare room had become my room and I appreciated it.

On my bedside table stood the mug that Mr Benson's sister had given me from her own pottery. I liked that she had said it was a bit wonky, so she'd give it to me. She was a plain-spoken woman. And there was nothing wrong with the mug.

I opened the drawer of the bedside table where I kept my treasures. There was the A-Z Maps of London, my Savings Book, my two Student Identity Cards and the credit note from the Gold Mart. I took out the Savings Bank Book and the Kingswell Student

Card that had my photo. I would take it along with me just in case. I stashed them in the inside pocket of my jacket.

I took a deep breath of pleasure at what I had decided to do. I needed to get on with it while my determination lasted. I went at once and cycled along to the Post Office. I was not sure of the procedure for taking money out as I had never done it before but I did feel confident that I would manage it. I recalled Mrs Robinson and all her doubts about me when I first came to Grandfather's house asking me whether I had any identification to prove who I was and I smiled to myself as I remembered showing her my school Library card. What a long time ago that seemed. I was not sure whether they would in fact be asking for proof of identity in the Post Office but if it turned out that they did, I was prepared. I felt a glow of satisfaction.

I chose the counter with a young woman and she smiled at me and asked how she could help me. I felt pleasantly nervous. I had never had to do anything like this before.

'I want to take some money out of my Savings Book' I said.

'Of course. Have you got your Savings Book with you?' she asked and I handed it over to her under the grid and she began to look at it.

She pushed a form over the counter to me.

'Put the date at the top. Fill in the amount you want to take out and sign the bottom with your usual signature' she said.

I filled in the slip to say that I wanted to take out £120, signed the bottom and passed it back to her.

'Have you got any identification?' she asked and I passed my student card under the grid also.

She read it and looked up at me comparing me with my photograph, checking my signature. I had not done such a transaction before. I almost expected her to ask me where I had got the money from and why I wanted to take some out. In a way, in fact, she did.

The young woman teller looked at me and smiled and asked quite casually what I wanted the money for. When I hesitated, thinking how I should answer her, she smiled and explained that she just wanted to check that no one was asking me for money or menacing me, so I smiled back at her and said no, no-one was threatening me, it was just for a second-hand lap-top computer that I had seen advertised and wanted to buy and which I could well do with. She was satisfied with that – and smiled and said, 'Well, be sure it's in working order if it's second hand. Maybe make an offer for it!' We smiled happily at each other. In a moment she was counting out the money. She stamped the transaction in the Savings Book and passed it back to me with the bank notes tucked inside it and my student identity card with it, and said 'Good luck.' I tucked it all safely into the inside pocket of my jacket.

'Thanks!' I said.

Mission accomplished, I thought. Or the first step of it.

***

I cycled along to Little Venice and located again where the Mary-Lou was berthed. I hailed the occupants. 'Hi,' I said. 'I hear you've got a computer to sell and I'd like to see it if I may.'

'Come aboard,' they welcomed me. I was grateful they didn't comment how young I looked nor ask whether I could afford it. I stepped aboard gingerly, not sure if it would rock like a boat, and that was a thrill in itself. I told them it was the first canal boat I had ever been on.

'We must show you round then,' they said.

They sat me down on a chair on the deck and gave me a cup of strong tea and a biscuit and brought out the lap-top. The lap-top was as like my own one from school as could be. They explained that they were moving their barge up-river, or up-canal more precisely, into a more country area and were divesting themselves of all the stuff they never used. They showed me round all the facilities on the barge, the table that became a small double bed, the galley kitchen, the stowaway cupboards. I could imagine myself living there, compact, everything to hand.

'Do you ever find it a bit public, living here with all the people just walking by on the pavement?' I asked.

'Not really. I never notice them,' the chap said.

'Well, I shall be glad to get somewhere quieter and more private,' she agreed with me.

'Actually, when you're sitting here on the cabin, you are less aware than you would think of the people outside the boat.'

'True.'

I found myself telling the couple all about Darren and how I was helping him with his difficulty in reading and his amazing propensity for maths and how I had lent him my lap-top but now I really needed to take it back for the lessons from my school as they were shortly to be streaming out to me again and my friend was showing a great reluctance to part with it and give it back. They were interested and said they would let it go for £100, it had its own case and they gave me a bag as well to carry it on my handlebars. I counted out the money, five twenty pound notes and thanked them and got up to go and we wished each other good luck.

'I hope you're happy with the computer. And that your friend takes to it.'   'I'm certain he will. And Thanks.'

When I got back to my bedroom, I took some time making as sure as I could be, that all the programmes Darren might need were on the new lap-top which seemed almost new and unused. I returned my Savings Book and Identity Card back to the drawer of the bedside table. I stuffed the spare twenty pound note into my trouser pocket. I was unused to having money and debated to myself whether I should put it back into the Savings Account but it seemed rather a complex manoeuvre almost as if I was trading.

I took myself over to Mrs Robinson's flat. Darren was asleep, having a nap, he seemed to need a lot of sleep as he recovered from his strains and bruises. His own computer, or rather my lap-top that Darren had been using, lay on the floor by the settee and I set about disconnecting it from the leads and began to pack it up, to find suddenly that Darren was awake and his eyes fixed on me.

'I know that you've got to take it back, mate,' he said. 'You're going to need it for your schoolwork that's streamed to you. But I shall really miss it, Spike. I was going to ask you, maybe you can bring it over at the weekends and I can catch up.'

'No need, Darren, I've bought you a present. Sit up!' And I put the new laptop in its case on Darren's knees.'

Darren was dumbfounded, took it out of the case and opened it up. His face was a picture. He said nothing. He could think of nothing to say.

'It's a present for you, Darren. But you've still got to keep reading with me! It's a laptop of your own and it's yours to keep. I simply *have* to take mine back. My school is streaming the next term's work shortly and I shall need it. But this one is for you. It's yours to keep.'

Darren looked at me wide-eyed. He shook his head. 'I can't believe it! I can't believe it! I can't believe it!'

He at once asked if I had half inched it.

'If you mean pinched,' I laughed, 'no, I paid for it. But actually, you're not far wrong because I used a bit of money that came from the Scrubs to buy it.'

'The Scrubs! Your Dad! 'said Darren. 'I shall treasure it all the more for knowing that. I hope you didn't pay full price.'

'No, I got them down to a hundred. They were asking one-twenty.'

'Spike, mate, I don't know what to say. You're a man after my own heart. You know, it was the best day of my life when I met you.'

We spent the next hour checking that the programmes were all there and available and transferring stuff across.

While we were in the midst of that, Mrs Robinson returned from one of her sallies. She was an indefatigable worker. She took on extra jobs from time to time to get by, she said. I noticed that she was carrying two great carrier bags of food and provisions, one in each hand, and I became aware that she was feeding Darren as well as herself. Darren was oblivious, unaware, too excited about his new possession.

'Auntie, come and look here. Spike's given me me own computer. I told you he would need to take his back and I was just asking him if he could bring it over maybe at the weekends so I could get on with my stuff and look! - he's come up with this!'

Mrs Robinson was taken aback. And more than a little hesitant as to whether they should accept it, wondering if it was from Mr Kingswell.

'No, it's not from him. It's from the Scrubs!' Darren said.

I had to reveal to Mrs Robinson that under the family photographs in the small metal box that my father had sent me to rescue, there had been some money. I didn't let on how much.

'I haven't told Grandfather about the money. Only the Photos. Alicia showed me how to put it into a Savings Bank,' I explained. 'I suppose it may not be mine eventually but meanwhile I feel justified to use some of it. It's in a good cause. And after all, I did lead Darren astray and cause his injuries.'

'Auntie will never accept that,' said Darren. 'She thinks I led you astray. But we both know it was the other way round. Who is Alicia anyway?'

I had to make a decision of how much to speak of things to Darren. After all, Mrs Robinson knew the complex relationships of the family. But she was not a great talker of other peoples' business. I decided to go halfway toward telling him.

'Who is Alicia? Well, I don't know how to tell you who she is. I really don't have the words for it. My grandfather tells me I could look on her like a cousin or like a sister. Alicia is his daughter.' And I produced one of the small photos of her that Alicia had had taken to apply for her Open University Course and she had given one to me. 'They were estranged for some years, my grandfather and his daughter.'

'I understand,' said Darren. 'In fact, I'm just the same, aren't I Auntie?' He looked at the photo. 'You do talk posh, Spike. Estranged. You mean they weren't talking. And actually, Spike, I'm exactly the same. My lot weren't talking either. My elder sister Julie is like an older sister to me and Julie's mother I called Mother, or I did before they were all not speaking, but really … well … it works if I call Julie my sister.'

'Tut, tut. Too much talk!' said Mrs Robinson. 'I'll get us all some tea and a piece of cake.'

I was aware once again that the small front room was rather overcrowded and wondered if I should take myself off.

'Mrs Robinson, you would tell me if I'm outstaying my welcome, wouldn't you? You must be tired of me always here, especially when you've just come in and wanting your tea, I can take myself off if you think I should go.'

'You can come and help me make the tea, Spike,' she said. 'We haven't tired of you yet.'

We left Darren with his new computer on his knees, learning his way round, lost to exploring. 'It's even got its own case,' he crowed, 'I'm right set up.'

Mrs Robinson and I busied ourselves in the kitchen making the tea which she said she could well do with.

'I saw it advertised from one of the canal barges, Mrs Robinson. They were nice people. It's quite genuine. They were asking 120 and I told them about Darren's need for the computer and how I had to take mine back for the on-line schoolwork streaming and they let it go for 100. If you won't be offended, I'll give you the other 20, Mrs Robinson, I can see you buying a great stash of stuff to feed Darren, and it really was my fault that he was injured, not his.'

I brought the twenty pound note out of my pocket and tucked it into the kitchen drawer where she kept her teaspoons. 'And don't forget, Mrs Robinson, I've had the use of the bike; I've been all over the place on that.'

She smiled. 'You're a caution, Spike,' she said to me. 'And I won't say no.'

Chapter 31

Persuasion

Grandfather was at last going to be allowed to meet with Darren to have his interview.

I viewed the negotiations with interest. It was clear that Mrs Robinson would have preferred Darren to meet with Mr Kingswell anywhere but in the sanctity of her flat. But Darren was only slowly getting back on his feet. She would have accepted a meeting over in Hamilton Terrace or anywhere else on her own estate—in fact, anywhere but in the front room of her home.

She agreed at last. She made it clear that she would not be entertaining Mr Kingswell, not even to a cup of tea. It meant something special to her, to have someone come into her flat and be given tea. She did not want that. I sort of understood how she felt. For hadn't I been given a royal welcome when invited to tea by her? Of course, Mr Kingswell did not feel the need for a cup of tea, but nor did he really begin to understand the nuance of her strong feelings of privacy and her proud ownership of her home. His visiting Darren there didn't have the same symbolic meaning to

Grandfather as it did for Mrs Robinson to allow him to enter her home. She herself, she said, would be hovering in the kitchen.

On the appointed day, I walked Grandfather over to the tower block, pointed out which was Baer Block, showed him where the entrance was, negotiated the lift for him, ushered him in and pressed the button for the 27th floor. I went with him along the walkway toward Mrs Robinson's front door, and once he heard the door chimes, I stood back and ushered him in. He propped himself quietly against the wall to the kitchen.

Darren was more or less a captive subject, still confined to the sofa bed. Grandfather stood before him. At first, Darren remained reluctant to communicate with him. This old man might be the grandfather of his friend Spike, but he equated him in his mind with a schoolteacher and felt defensive about any inroads or discussion.

Grandfather went to sit down on the one chair.

Darren spoke. 'That's Auntie's chair.'

Grandfather said mildly, 'It is indeed.' Then, after a bit, he said, 'I am very sorry my grandson has led you into this scrape and laid you up with injuries.'

'It's nothing. Think nothing of it. Spike's my mate.'

'Hear me out, Darren. You have a very unusual brain. You're very, very clever at numbers—very clever indeed—and good at spatial logical thinking. That is, planning where things relate to each other and where they should go. I think, given some help on the letters and reading, you will be able to make great strides in mathematics and quite possibly engineering. It would be a pity, with an exceptional brain like yours, to refuse to develop it. With a little help, you could have a great future—in engineering, say. You would enjoy it. And make good money.'

'Go along with you!' said Darren. 'I'm no good at book learning.'

'I'm here, in fact, because I should like to put you in the book I am writing. And I need your permission to do that. I need to monitor and record the advances you make—but I should need to come and meet with you occasionally, maybe once a week, and give you some special tasks to do. Well, you're a captive audience here, so you might as well humour an old man. I need your permission. And, you know, I can do something for you in return.

'Once you're on your feet again, I have looked into a place for you to do your maths. It's a sixth form college you might go to. Not full-time. To start with, just to attend the mathematics class with older boys.'

'They're all shut down, aren't they? Like Spike's school. With the virus epidemic.'

'Well, that's not quite true. They are still open for boys from… well, whose parents are working in… well, there are some limited classes going on.' He didn't like to say that they were open for

Special Needs children as well as a smattering of the children of key workers.

Darren looked at him. He was unsure whether to believe him. He was right to be suspicious.

Grandfather was being somewhat economical with the truth. With his academic position and connections, he had found it possible to make enquiries and to get answers about the current position on schooling and access to classes. He was not interested in hearing details about the reasons for Darren's repeated suspensions and exclusions. Darren needed to make a fresh start.

A teacher had been found who was said to be inspirational in higher mathematics—algebra and calculus. He taught in a sixth form college. Unfortunately, the sixth form college where he had found a suitable slot for Darren was attached to a school from which Darren had indeed been excluded in the past. But the college itself was in a porta-cabin that was separated a little from the main school buildings, and perhaps Darren would not identify it too closely in his mind as one from which he had already been banished.

It was only the maths classes he would be enrolled in, and the name *Kingswell* had been sufficient to open some doors for him. He had found a possible place for Darren and had given the injuries as a reason for his request for part-time attendance.

Now he pointed out to Darren how important it was that he continued to work also on improving his literacy—his reading—

because he would need to read the words and understand instructions: those words that explained what was needed to solve each maths problem. It opens doors, he explained.

It was clearly risky, Grandfather realised, whether Darren was going to be prepared to give it a try. But to get him into his project, he thought it was a risk worth taking. It was important that Darren give consent to be included as a subject in papers and presentations, even though his name would not be given.

I said nothing, playing dumb, propped up against the wall. Nor did Darren look over to me. He had to make up his own mind and commitment.

'What do you say?' Grandfather asked eventually, after explaining all he could, giving Darren the choice of accepting or refusing. He held out toward him a sheaf of test papers in a transparent folder with a couple of pencils stuck in the top. 'Give it a go. You might start with these test papers. Then, if you can manage them, we'll see if Spike can walk you round there to the maths class.'

That was the first I had heard about that!

Darren looked at them and slowly held out his hand. 'Go on then!' he said. 'Let's give it a go!'—and took the test papers.

He told me afterwards that it was the brand-new pencils sticking out from the top of the sheaf of papers that made him decide to take part.

Chapter 32

Elsie

I was to be roped in as the escort to walk Darren along to the Sixth Form College.

Mrs Robinson and the Probation Officer contrived to provide a pair of walking sticks, and we got Darren up from the couch. He was stiff at first and groaned, but he had to admit it was good to be on his feet. We spent a few days—Darren and I—making practice walks around the estate, patrolling the stretches of featureless cement between the tower blocks. He was really ropy at walking at first, but within a few days, Darren, being such a fit boy, was progressing to using only one stick and regaining his mobility.

The class he was to join was at eleven o'clock, after the morning break, and I took Darren over. We were met at the entrance by the maths teacher. He had been alerted and forewarned after Mr Kingswell had made contact.

Seeing the walking stick and the escort, he didn't make any facetious comments, just said nicely, "You're coming to join us, are you? Let's see if you can follow what we're up to in this class. Speak up if you want any explanations. Maybe just listen at first and see if you can follow. Your friend can sit at the back and wait to walk you home after."

I could see, in his mind's eye, that he felt doubtful whether this tough-looking boy—young in age for his class, hobbling in with a walking stick—was going to cope with his maths group. I went quietly to sit at the back. I watched Darren join the group. There were five or six older lads and, to my surprise, two girls. One of the girls, seeing Darren's limp and walking stick, made a place next to her for Darren to sit at a table where he could stretch his leg out and prop up the stick.

The class began. The teacher distributed papers he had prepared for the lesson—one for each student—pages full of problems with gaps for the answers. Darren said nothing, but it was an area that he had already touched on in his new online programme. The teacher spoke for five minutes or so in explanation. Darren listened intently, and then they were left to get on with the first problem on the paper. I saw the teacher glance across to see 'the new boy' filling in numbers with his pencil on the sheet. He gave them all time to do it—twenty minutes or so.

"If you're stuck, speak up and I'll come round," he said, giving a helping hand to one or two.

"Now swap the papers with the student next to you and mark each other's papers." They all exchanged the paper sheets. He went through the answers and asked for the scores.

"He's got them all right," said the girl, handing back Darren's work. "I know I haven't got them all done. I got stuck on number five and then couldn't manage the next one. Would you go over that with us all again and explain?" she said.

The teacher held out his hand for their papers. A glance showed him it was, as she said—the new boy had produced a correct set of answers. The teacher did not quite seem ready as yet to confront this situation and needed time to deal with it. He drummed with his fingers on the desk.

"Well done," he said. He turned to the girl. "Get your neighbour to show you his workings on numbers five and six while I explain over here."

And he moved across to talk through the concept to the lads at the next table.

****

At the end of the class—an hour and a half of further maths, quite intensive work—the teacher dished out the homework sheets.

I watched from the back and saw Darren looking at the words at the top of the page, and I could imagine they probably confirmed his worst fears. Quite possibly he could make neither head nor tail of them. Maybe, I thought, he would ask me later to see if he would be able to read and understand the instructions.

Then I watched as Darren solved his own problem. As the girl next to him started to get up and leave, Darren seized the moment and delayed her with a hand on her arm.

"Can you just read this for me?" he said.

He jabbed his finger at the introductory text.

"Of course," she said, and sat down again.

She rattled off the instructions.

"Slowly, please. And point with your finger at what you're reading," he said.

"Sorry."

She did as he asked.

"Could I trouble you to do that once more?" he said. "What's your name?"

"Elsie," she said, and read it again.

The teacher was coming over to see what was going on.

"Next lesson, tomorrow, is at eleven again, but we may change the times so keep aware of that. Did you follow? Did you keep up?"

Darren heaved himself up. "It was fine," he said. "I'll be here tomorrow. I hope my mate will be able to come and walk back with me. I'm only just on my pins again."

"What happened to you?"

"It's a long story," said Darren, aware that if he described what really happened it would sound as though he was a cat burglar.

He was clearly relieved to find me propped up against the wall waiting outside.

"How did it go?" I asked.

"It was OK," said Darren. "This is Elsie."

"Hi."

"Hi." She shouldered her backpack and went off with a flutter of her hand.

"I've got some homework to do. That was Elsie, by the way. We shared a table. I got her to read the words of the homework for me, but it'd be good if you could just go over the words again with me. It's quite right what your grandfather said—I need to get the reading better so I can understand the instructions for the maths."

"We'll work on it. You are already loads better than where you were a few weeks ago. We'll just keep pegging away at it."

I got him back home to his auntie's flat. He flopped onto the sofa and put his feet up. His leg was aching and he took two paracetamol with water. He shut his eyes.

I quickly looked at the instruction and printed one or two words in large, simple letters for him and said, "I've got to go, Darren. I've got to connect up for the online streaming of my own schoolwork. The term's work has begun again. I'll be back later this afternoon."

****

The weeks flew by. At last, restrictions were going to be lifted and Ranford School was set to re-open. There were going to be strict arrangements for testing for the virus each time the boys entered the school: testing, waiting an hour for the result, and being let in once given the all-clear.

Of course, I was eager to get back into school, but I was also concerned about Darren continuing with his reading practice. Grandfather went over once a week to collect the previous week's test papers, which enabled him to chart the progress Darren was making. Each time, he gave him a new set of papers to work on. I remained worried that, without the daily slog of practice reading with me, Darren's literacy would not maintain its improvement.

I went over to Baer Tower to say a temporary goodbye before I went back to school. I found him in high spirits.

'I only just got back from me Maths class, Spike. You'd never guess what I've bin doing. I've bin doin' a bit of teaching at the main school with ole Erbie.'

Old Herbie! That's what they were calling their maths tutor. Why, he didn't explain, but Darren was clearly at ease and had got dug in with the group.

'They asked 'im to take a class at the main school – the one that threw me out.'

It was the first time I realised that Darren had become aware that the Sixth Form class he was attending was part of a school that had excluded him in the past.

'He said it was a right difficult mob he had been asked to teach, and he couldn't get them to listen to him and pay attention. I think, with all this lockdown, things had got out of hand. They were meant to be working for an exam, but they wouldn't settle down. I offered to go along with him. I can walk quite well on my own now, but I still take my stick.'

Darren said the tutor had been a bit taken aback at his offer, but they had strolled over together, talking all the while. Darren was always at ease talking to people.

'We walked into the classroom together, me with my stick. There was a great hubbub of noise. The children were all moving around, jumping up and down, sitting on top of the desks, shoving and jostling each other. I took one look at them and I saw at once a trio of troublemakers.

'"Sit at your desks," I commanded. They were so shocked that they obeyed and shuffled into their seats. I told them how fortunate they were to have the opportunity to learn some maths from one of the best teachers in the school.

'One of the troublemakers made a sneering noise, like they do — "Yeah-eh" — and his friend hunched his shoulders and giggled. I took one step toward the boy who had smirked and told him I hoped he wasn't so stupid as not to want to learn anything, and I glared at him. He ducked his head and stifled any further remark. His ears went red — that's always a good sign.'

Apparently, Darren had gone and leant against the wall near the door and the tutor had launched into his lesson. He was a good teacher and had engaged the interest of the class, and by the end of the lesson, he had them eating out of his hand—listening, responding, answering questions thrown out.

Darren said he avoided looking at any of the troublesome trio. They had settled down. He simply ignored them from then on.

As they walked away together—Darren stomping along with his stick—the tutor had said he had one question for Darren: how did he know how to handle them?

Darren said, 'I told him. I told him. I told him. I used to be one of them.'

****

Darren, telling me that, gave me confidence in myself once I was back in school. Mr Benson had put me in charge of supervising the young boys in a library session after their early lunch and before their break-time and afternoon lessons.

They were meant to read in the library for half an hour after lunch, before they were free and allowed out to the grounds to play. Most of them did nothing—not reading a book, just waiting for release. They mooched around, waiting to be let out.

If Darren could do it, I thought, I would give it a try. I approached one big fellow, sitting on top of a desk, chewing at the knuckle of his hand.

'You look to me like a *Biggles* reader,' I said. '*Biggles* is a hero, gets into all sorts of trouble, and always manages to get himself out of it.'

I handed him a *Biggles* book. 'Tell me what you make of him!'

He slid off the desk onto a chair and started on the first page.

I approached a thin, small boy blinking behind spectacles.

'Do you like stars and the universe?' I asked him. 'Or do you prefer biology, plants, or animals?'

'Actually, I like anatomy,' he said. 'Bones and the body. I'm going to be a doctor.'

I fished out an interesting-looking book on scientific discoveries—a chapter on Watson and Crick and the Double Helix, one on heart surgery, and another on transplants.

'I'll give it a go,' he said.

Some of the others were gathering around now, waiting on me to give suggestions. I got them all matched with a book to suit their interests.

At the end, when the bell went to let them out, the big fellow made no rush to go, immersed in an exploit with *Biggles*.

I didn't think I could match Darren's mastery, but I did get them all usefully engaged on one book or another—not just mooching around waiting to be let out.

****

I need not have worried about Darren persevering with his reading practice. Elsie had become quite a chum, and while they did their maths together—and Darren helped her with it—she was also willing to sit alongside him on the sofa-bed and guide him through his reading practice. He was always going to stumble over reading and spelling, but he had already progressed to the point where he could enjoy some of the boys' adventure books I had hoped he would reach.

Chapter 33

Half-Term

Ranford School re-opened. We boys were all back at school. After a few days, it was as though we had never left. We felt we were being swamped with schoolwork to make up for the time we had lost. It was a pleasure to be back with regular lessons.

I did notice, though, that for me, there was now a subtle difference. School had been my only home and family. While it still was home and family to me, I was subtly aware that I now had another home as well—and a bit of a new family. Or so I believed. Or so I hoped.

Until—

Until it came to the first exeat. It was a long one. Half-term. A whole week at home.

I was beginning to feel a little unsure. A coach was to be laid on, as usual, to take boys from the main gates to the station after lunch on Friday. Was I to pack a small bag and join the rest of the departing boys? Could I assume I was expected in Hamilton Terrace? I was assailed by doubt.

The last time I had taken that coach and then the train, I had made up an emergency pack and spent the night as a homeless boy in the open air, in my sleeping bag in Lincoln's Inn Fields. I didn't intend to repeat that. But how sure could I be that Grandfather was expecting me? For the life of me, I could not remember whether we had made any definite arrangements.

Returning to school had all been rather uncertain, with the results of repeat testing determining whether a boy would be allowed back in or not. In fact, we had all tested negative, and school had resumed as near normal as possible.

I went and stood outside my Housemaster's room, debating whether to knock on the door and ask Mr Benson's advice as to what he thought I should do. Should I just turn up and hope for the best—and assume my room was still there for me? If Grandfather expressed surprise to see me—if I was turned away—should I go to see if Mrs Robinson would make good her offer of the sofa-bed in her flat in the tower block?

I knew, of course, that I could not—because it had already been claimed by her nephew and was being occupied by Darren. I was full of doubt. I went over and over it in my mind. Did I think Grandfather would be expecting me? Could I assume he would be ready to receive me again?

I thought I knew what my Housemaster, Mr Benson, would say. He would ask me, *What arrangements did you make before you left?* For the life of me, I really did not know what we had talked about, or what had been arranged.

While I stood there dithering, plagued by uncertainty, wondering whether to knock on the Housemaster's door or not, Mrs Clarke, the Headmaster's wife, came by.

'Oh, Sebastian,' she said, 'I wanted to have a word with you. Now is a good time. Come and have tea with me in the Headmaster's study.'

My heart sank. I anticipated already what she was going to say. I feared there was only one reason she would want to have a word with me. She was even giving me tea to soften the blow. I was fearful she would say I was expected to stay in school over the exeat. I imagined she was going to tell me that Grandfather was old and could not be expected to continue looking after me—and was not willing to have me back.

I remembered my statement to Mrs Robinson: *I was no trouble, was I?*—and her insistence that it was very, very good of Mr Kingswell to put me up. I had taken for granted that we had got along together in a harmonious way—but perhaps that was not how Grandfather had experienced it. If the Head's wife wanted to speak to me, the outlook looked gloomy.

We went through the Headmaster's study to her little sitting room beyond, and she ordered tea. It came promptly with buttered, toasted tea-cakes. She poured the tea and invited me to tuck in.

'Now, I wanted to ask you, Sebastian, how you felt about staying with your Kingswell grandfather. It was very enterprising of you to arrange that all by yourself—and I won't go over the importance of always letting us at school know where you are! But that is water under the bridge. It was resourceful of you. Nonetheless, I wanted to ask you, completely confidentially, how you found it there, and whether you were completely happy. If you have any concerns at all, please tell me now.' She repeated, 'Any concerns at all.'

She fixed her eyes on me. She had a powerful gaze. It was not possible to tell her anything but the truth.

'It was wonderful, Mrs Clarke. How he lives and studies and writes and works is just how I like to live—and we were looked after by Mrs Robinson, the lady who "does" for him. You know, ever since I came here to Ranford, this school has been my home and my family, and I was bereft when it closed. It still is my home and my family. But I did find a second home and family with Grandfather Kingswell.'

I was going to go on to say that I knew he was old, and if it was all too much for him and he didn't want me back, I would try to understand. But before I could form the words, she went on.

'That's good, then. I just wanted to clear that up—in case you had any considerations that you needed to voice with me. He's been on the phone to me, asking the times when you're coming back, and I wanted to give you the opportunity to voice any problems.'

I was gobsmacked.

The news that Grandfather had been on the phone to enquire when I would be coming back—that he was expecting me to join him—swamped me with happiness. I could hardly speak for relief, and I stuttered a question to be sure.

'He phoned you, then? He *is* expecting me?' I could not keep the relief and joy out of my voice.

She nodded.

When I could speak again, I said, 'Thank you, Mrs Clarke. It makes me very happy to hear he is expecting me and wants me back. Actually, I wanted to thank you too, Mrs Clarke, for your help toward the prison visit. It went more or less smoothly, thanks to you.'

And then I found myself telling her all about the visit and how neither Grandfather nor I could spot, for one awful moment, which prisoner—among the line of men seated behind each table—was ours to visit.

She laughed.

'A surreal moment!' she said—whatever that means. But she did find it funny.

She told me that my father might quite probably be moved to an open prison in the future, which might be further away—in Suffolk, perhaps—but she would let me and Grandfather know when she heard any news.

'I don't expect a release before you finish school here, in fact,' she said. 'So school must continue to be home and family to you. You are well settled in your House, I believe. Mr Benson was a good choice as your Housemaster, I think.'

I agreed fervently and embarked on telling her of the half-term experience that I and three other boys from the House had enjoyed—trout fishing in the Grampians. She had learned something of that already from our various descriptions of what we had done during the break.

I decided against telling her that I had gone back up to Scotland to retrieve Mr Benson's school files that he had left behind there. I decided, too, not to tell the story of the retrieval of the little metal box—its contents, the photographs, and most particularly, the money that was now deposited in a savings account in my name. Nor would I say that I had already dipped into it to buy a laptop for a friend. The second metal box was still a mystery.

Nor would I mention that I had met Alicia. There were some things that I could share and tell, and other things that were best kept to oneself.

The toasted tea-cakes were finished now, and I had already had a third cup of tea. For some reason—perhaps remembering my talks with Mrs Robinson and hearing all about her family, and then finding I was capable of holding a similar conversation with Annie of Room 4A about her family—I felt able to ask Mrs Clarke if she had any plans herself for the long exeat week.

'I do indeed, Sebastian,' she said. 'I am planning to have my daughter's two children to stay. She is on her own with them; she works, so holiday time is always difficult for her.'

I was surprised. I hadn't imagined her with grown-up children and grandchildren.

'How old are they?' I asked.

She told me—a grandson of eight and a granddaughter of seven.

'How marvellous for them that they each have a sister and brother,' I said, and she smiled and agreed how important that was, and that she would remember to tell them that when they embarked on any arguments or fights with each other.

'I shall tell them you said how fortunate they were to have each other.'

Then I found myself telling her that I had made a very good friend while living with Grandfather, and told her a little about Darren, who lived on Mrs Robinson's estate, his problem with not being able to read, and his brilliance at mathematics. She was interested and said I must let her know how he was getting along.

I thanked her for the tea and told her it was the second time I had been invited out to tea, and told her a little about having tea with Mrs Robinson on the 27th floor of the Tower Block.

'It's been nice to talk with you,' she said. 'And have a good time at the exeat.'

I felt I had made another friend.

Chapter 34

Tony

Grandfather was snoozing in the leather armchair in his study when I walked in.

The front door had been left on the latch for me. I dumped my pack on the ground and put my hand on his shoulder.

'I'm home, Grandfather!' I said.

Grandfather opened his eyes.

'So I see,' he said. 'Welcome home.'

****

Grandfather told me he had been making great inroads on writing his latest book.

'These things always take much longer than you think they will,' he said, 'but on this occasion, I am soaring ahead with it.'

Once a week, Grandfather had been walking over to the Estate to assess progress. On his return, he made notes on his A4 block of paper to record the landmarks that Darren had reached—particularly in reading, as well as in mathematics and logical thinking.

The strange, eccentric way that Darren's intelligence had developed had been a welcome fillip to the Kingswell research and writing. Grandfather continued to set the weekly tests for Darren to complete. The previous week's test papers were eagerly retrieved. Once received, Grandfather entered the results into tables and charts and plotted them on his graphs.

Largely unbeknown to Darren, his reading development would illuminate Grandfather's latest book as a practical example. It would be projected on PowerPoint at international meetings. It would add confirmation to his theories of how the mind worked—of how intelligence develops, sometimes in a lopsided manner. It was all part of his study into the effect of education on the individual and on society.

We had a pleasant supper together—a meal that Mrs Robinson had prepared for us. Grandfather talked about his book and his writings. We read the latest letter with news from Alicia.

I told Grandfather about being invited for tea and toasted tea-cakes with Mrs Clarke. I didn't reveal how fearful I had been, how unsure I had felt about whether or not I could just assume I was welcome back with him. In fact, I had almost forgotten that fear already, now it was resolved. But I made him laugh as I told him how she had persistently called me Sebastian and wanted to know if I had any concerns about going back to Grandfather Kingswell. *Any concerns at all.*

He laughed, but then became serious and said it was splendid that she had been checking to make sure things were alright.

'After all,' Grandfather said, 'I am an old reprobate, a recluse according to your Housemaster, an eccentric who has lost both a wife and a daughter without realising they had gone—and who ought to have some regrets about that. So I am fortunate that an old fellow like me has been lucky enough to have a grandson—one he didn't even know he had—descend on him to keep him company. And who has introduced a friend of his, a boy who will illuminate his research and writings as a fascinating subject for study.'

'Nonsense, Grandfather,' I said. 'You're not a recluse. And Darren is a good mate, not just a subject for study. He is an incredibly brave chap, and together we—you and I—have done as many good things for him as he has helped you by being a feature in your writings.'

'You'll want to be checking on Darren, I know. But I thought of one more thing you could do this week while you are here at home. I thought you might like to check on Tony—your other grandfather who brought you up—and see if he is alright.'

'I will, Grandfather. I shall need to think about how to go about doing that, though. Ideally, I would use the bike to get myself there, and I see the bike is still here in the hall. I'll try and get over to see Tony tomorrow, before I hear that Darren is so far recovered that he is able to pedal again and wants his bike back.'

I went and brought down the tattered A–Z book from my room, and we looked up a route back to my childhood home.

'On a bike, it should not take me too long.'

Then I had a further thought about the mechanics of making a visit.

'Do you think I can just turn up, Grandfather, or do I need to check with him first?'

Grandfather thought I should just turn up—realising that Tony, having written rather vehemently that he was no longer prepared to look after me, might well make some excuse that it was inconvenient to see me. But if I turned up with something in my hand, he was unlikely to turn me away.

'He will be surprised to see you. You have probably changed a good bit—even in appearance—after... how long since you last saw him?'

'It must be three years now. Maybe four. Three years plus, since the day my father got Pat to spruce me up and took me to see the Headmaster at Ranford School—and they took me in right away. I had no uniform or anything, and my father had no spare time to shop for the kit, as he was due in court the next day. I remember Mrs Clarke took control and said, "Say goodbye to your father, Sebastian, and we'll go and find your Housemaster." And that was that.'

'And you never saw Pat and Tony again? Putting yourself in their shoes, Spike, they might have felt a bit put out that this child they had looked after for twelve years or so had been whisked away without a by-your-leave or a thank you. I'm not criticising your father, Spike—and he must have been in a difficult position—but let us hope he did thank them graciously and explain what he was doing and why.'

'Oh dear! Who knows what passed between them. Well—if I go, what shall I take for Tony?'

'I suggest half of the cake that Mrs Robinson has baked to welcome you home! It's very large, and we'll never manage to eat it all.'

'I'll take a slab of it. Half is maybe too much.'

****

My childhood home, where I had grown up with Pat and Tony, looked both familiar and a bit down-at-heel when I cycled up to it, wheeled my bike inside the front gate, and propped it up against the hedge. I didn't think too much about what I was going to say.

I rang the doorbell and knocked with the knocker. When I had last been there, I had only just been tall enough to reach that doorknocker, which was a rather nice brass knobbly shape like a fist.

Tony shouted at once in answer to the knock, 'The door's on the latch. I'm in the garden. Come through to the back.'

I wondered who he thought I was, ringing the bell and knocking at the door. Perhaps a neighbour. Or a friend.

I pushed open the front door—dark green, 'forest green' he had called it. Tony was always very precise. The paint was now worn and peeling a little. The hall was narrow and small, musty. Tony's coat and trilby hat were hanging on the first peg. Alongside it, the peg where Pat's coat had hung stood stark and empty.

I went through to the kitchen, which led to the garden. The sink was piled with dishes waiting to be washed up. I wondered if I should tidy the place. I could see him through the glass of the back door, bent over his runner beans and fruit bushes. The apple tree hung heavy with fruit. My old swing dangled from a branch of the oak. The grass on the lawn looked as though it needed the mower run over it—the edges not trimmed.

I stepped onto the paving stones outside the back door and called his name.

'Tony, it's me. Seb. Sebastian. I've brought some cake. Shall I put the kettle on?'

He turned slowly and shielded his eyes with his hand against the sunlight to look at me.

'Seb? Is it really you? You've grown! Well—of course.'

I walked across the grass to him. Tony was never a man of many words. Nor a man given to affectionate gestures. I stretched out my hand to him and grasped his—gnarled knuckles and dry.

'How are you? How have you been?'

What else was there to say? I could see how he was. Older. Sadder. Keeping going. Still fairly silent.

'I saw Dad,' I told him. 'I did a prison visit. Just a few months ago.'

Tony's face contorted a little, his mouth twisting. 'How was he?'

'Changed, of course. Prison haircut. No—the same. He asked me to do a job for him.'

'I imagine,' he chuckled. 'Typical. Did you do it?'

'I did. It was OK. Not too difficult.'

He shrugged. He could see I was not being open with him.

'Look, let's have that tea,' he said. 'We'll have it on this little round table on the terrace. Give me a moment to get my bearings.'

I went inside and lit the gas under the kettle. There was no hot water in the tap, so I filled the kettle right up and, as soon as it was warm, used it to fill the basin in the sink for the washing-up, then filled the kettle again with fresh water. I set to, put everything to rights, and tidied the place up.

I went to the refrigerator for the milk and had never seen a fridge so empty. Mrs Robinson's cake was a very necessary addition to the mugs of tea.

As we sat on the two metal chairs round the small garden table and drank the tea, he really tucked into the cake. I realised I should have brought half the cake—or more.

'I gather school has worked out well for you,' he said.

'It has. It was the best decision my father ever made to put me in there.'

'Well, I'm glad for that. Pat would be pleased that you are secure there. Thank you for the note you wrote when she died.'

'I'm so sorry that she was ill and died. You and Pat were very good to me all those years through my childhood.'

A silence fell on us then. It was as though we had nothing else to say to each other—though in fact there was much else we needed to say.

'Tony, you don't look as though you are looking after yourself.'

'I get by. I get by. I just have my own pension to get by on, and it's not a lot to live on. And the house goes to rack and ruin with neglect. There's always something that needs doing. I'm just glad that Pat isn't here to see us not coping. She would have deserved much better than this. She always had a little job as well as what I earned, and we should have been comfortable. But—there it is! At least we had paid off the mortgage years ago. I have to be grateful for that. We always put something by for the future, you know, both Pat and me.'

'I remember. You always had your Savings, Tony.'

Tony looked at me solemnly.

'Sebastian, we gave it all to your father. Both Pat and I did. He was desperate, and he felt sure he could pay us back when he turned things round. But we had the money in the bank, and it didn't seem right not to lend it to him.'

I felt a cold hand settle on the nape of my neck and then descend like a stream down the vertebrae of my spine.

'How awful! How awful, Tony! How much did you lend him? You and Pat?'

'He cleared us out. Mine and Pat's. I did say at the time that Pat should have kept something back, but she was adamant that she wanted to do as much for him as I was doing. I think she believed that he would pay us back. But I can see that he never would be able to turn things round now. I sell the odd thing in the house occasionally, when a bill comes up that I can't meet. You'll see when you go round the house.'

We sat and talked, recalling happy times from my childhood, and I was able to tell him what good memories I had and thank him for the way that he and Pat had made a home for me.

Quite casually, I was able to ask him the amount that they had lent to my father. I was bearing in mind the notes that had lain under the photographs—but they were nowhere near equivalent. Such large sums meant little to me, as I had no experience of handling large amounts of money. It seemed to me, at a rough guess, that Tony and Pat had parted with their life savings—probably what amounted to something like two hundred and forty thousand pounds.

The notes in the little metal box, which had seemed a lot to me—five hundred pounds—represented only a tiny fraction of what was owed to Tony and Pat. I could hardly work it out. The notes in the little metal box would need to be replicated something approaching five hundred times in order to repay what they had lost.

He gave one further insight into what wholesome, straightforward, and honest people both Pat and Tony had been. He said that Pat had just kept one small sum in a Savings Book, which she intended to give to me, her only grandson, when she had given the rest of her savings away.

'I have tried not to use it, knowing that she wanted you to have something from both of us, but once or twice things have got desperate and I have had to dip into it.'

Now was not the time to tell him bluntly to use it. I realised I must deal with the situation with sensitivity.

I didn't ask him who he had been expecting when he called out that the door was on the latch and to let myself in. Perhaps it had been a friendly neighbour who, seeing the bike and hearing us talk, had decided not to intrude.

We had a good chat, and I said I would call again. I put the remnants of the cake back into his kitchen and said how glad I was to have made contact again.

****

Grandfather was intrigued to know how we had got on. Without dwelling on the empty larder, I described the visit. Grandfather's main concern was that it had been friendly.

'Absolutely,' I told him. 'No recriminations on either side.'

I did mention to Grandfather that I thought they had given away substantial amounts of their savings to their son.

'I do realise now, Grandfather, that that was why he had written to the school to say that he could no longer look after me. He didn't have the funds to do so. I will let Mr Benson and Mrs Clarke from school know that I believe that was the reason behind his statement—because they had said at the time that they were a little taken aback at the vehemence with which he had written.'

I had some decisions to make now. One was who I could discuss the whole situation with. I did need to talk it through with someone who would understand.

I went through the list of people I knew and trusted and could use as a sounding board. In my mind, I listed Grandfather himself, Mrs Clarke the Headmaster's wife, my Housemaster Mr Benson, and Mrs Robinson. I drew a line after those four.

There was also Alicia, Mary Benson, and Dr Hendricks. There was Darren. That seemed to be the total of my acquaintances—unless I counted the inhabitants of Little Great Middleton Street: Annie, now in the Old People's Home in the Mile End Road; Alf, who gave out the evening newspapers at the tube station with his little mute child; Eric, living away from his two wives; and the Heavies.

The other problem was to think what I could do to get adequate funds into Tony's bank account to enable him to live with dignity.

To my surprise, Mrs Robinson came near the top of my list of people with whom I could talk about things.

****

Meeting Mrs Robinson had, of course, been an experience in itself. It seemed to me that she knew about life. The generosity with which she shared her opinions was pure gold to me. There was no beating about the bush with Mrs Robinson. She pointed out things I would not have appreciated without her words. She increased my understanding of the way life was.

Her easy acceptance of the fact that my father was in prison was a reassurance that these things do happen—that it was a normality. She had even offered me the sofa-bed in her front room if I should ever need it. Having seen Darren confined to that sofa-bed for weeks, I hoped I would never have to take her up on that offer, but it did give me the security of another place where I was welcome. And, of course, knowing Mrs Robinson had led to Darren.

My comradeship with Darren was a friendship that had meant a great deal to me. I had enormous respect for him—his gung-ho courage, his get-up-and-go attitude to life.

I would not forget his quick, spontaneous offer to come with me and look over the site of my adventure, nor his lack of complaints when it all went wrong. His humour as we lay on the ground, trapped under the rubble—'Say, Spike, lucky you moved the bike.' The way he bore pain and injuries, never complaining. Nor had he blamed me for the fact that he had been unable to walk or get around for weeks on end. He had a great acceptance of life, of things that happened. Misfortune meant nothing to him. I suppose he rather expected things to go wrong and was not daunted when they did.

I felt great satisfaction that I had been able to help Darren change the direction of his life. Here was a boy not much older than I, a boy who could not read. Illiterate—I didn't even like to say the word. He was actually clever, street-wise, funny, a good bloke, and he could hardly read at all. He was such good company. And—illiterate, if that was the word—with all that literacy meant for his future. Now, by sheer chance, the fact that we had met, and, of course, not forgetting the hard work he had put in, he was learning to read as fluently as possible, and was achieving that without embarrassment or shame.

Nor did I forget that he had lent me his bike. The generous loan of that bike had enabled me to ride all over London in spite of lockdown. So it was with a little self-satisfaction that I had dropped by to check on Darren.

I was shocked to find that he was not there.

The sofa-bed had reverted to being a settee.

There was no sign of its late occupant.

****

Mrs Robinson greeted me with warmth.

'Oh, you're back! It's nice of you to drop by and say hello. I'll be seeing you later when I come by your grandfather's. I'd offer you a cup of tea, but I must be off in a minute to a little job I've got. You can walk with me if you will. It's just at the far side of the Estate.'

We walked together, and I hoped I concealed the fact that it was Darren in particular whom I had come to see, rather than just dropping in on her. After a bit, she volunteered news of Darren.

'Darren is back to near normal—walking and getting around, you'll be glad to hear. He comes over once a week to collect his tasks from Mr Kingswell and give him back the previous homework to mark. It was very good of Mr Kingswell to arrange for him to be taken on at the Sixth Form College. You know, he has a girlfriend now who does the reading with him. A very nice girl. It will be the making of him if she sticks with him.'

'I think I've met her,' I said. 'Elsie, is it? From the Maths class.'

'Elsie it is.' Then, after a pause, she added, 'You mustn't mind if he spends all his time with the girlfriend. That's the nature of things.'

'Just so long as he's reading, I suppose.'

'He seems to be. I had another thought about the Scrubs money that you used when you bought Darren that computer. I don't know how much the Scrubs money was, and I don't need to know, but it occurred to me that you could buy yourself a bike with that. The only problem is that you would have to tell your grandfather about it—which you haven't done, I gather.'

'I've no problem in telling Grandfather now that there was money in the metal box under the photographs. I'm not sure whether the money is mine, of course. What do you think?'

'I haven't met your father to form a judgement, but I imagine he would be agreeable to your using the money for a bike to get around.' She thought a bit further, then added, 'What he wouldn't want is obvious, Spike—drugs, alcohol, wine, women and song, and all that. But that's not you anyway. He wouldn't want you to splash it around either. When he comes out, he will need something to get started again, but who knows what provision he has made for himself. You also need to be on your guard as to who is aware that you have your Dad's money and how much. You won't mind my asking, did Alicia ask you for any?'

'No. No, certainly not. We counted it together and she advised me to put it into a Savings Account, which I did.'

'Quite right. Well, that's my advice. Tell your Grandfather that there were some notes under the photographs and you put it into a Savings Account and you'd like to use some to buy a bike—does he agree? I think the fewer people who know about its existence or the extent of it, the better.'

'Thanks, Mrs Robinson.'

That seemed to close down one avenue for further discussion. She had given her opinion.

I would drop over with Grandfather when he went for his weekly meeting with Darren, so that I could just make contact with Darren again. But it did seem that Darren had transferred his allegiance to the girlfriend, Elsie, and she would take on the reading project. Good luck to him.

Chapter 35

The Gold Mart

Back at Hamilton Terrace, there was a letter for me. A tattered, grubby white envelope with the stamp askew in the corner. For once, I opened it using a sharp knife to slit it neatly open. The paper inside was flimsy and thin, and I drew it out with care. I guessed at once where it was from—a letter from The Gold Exchange, the little shop like an opium den in the Charing Cross Road where I had deposited the larger of the two metal boxes, heavy with ancient coins, not all of the realm.

I gently unfolded the thin paper to reveal its message and smoothed its surface. The letter was poorly typed on what had clearly been an old typewriter, with lots of letters jumping above the lines on the page, some in heavy print, some faint, and all on the thin paper. I understood that. I appreciated that the owner of the Gold Mart was an eccentric old fellow, deeply knowledgeable on his own subject of interest, and it was obvious he had many contacts.

In the letter, he apologised for not being in touch earlier. He wrote that he was now aware of the provenance of the collection. If he understood correctly, he wrote, I was agreeable to deposit all the coins in the large metal box with him, to keep or to trade. He added that there were many coins in this splendid collection that were of special importance. Some were coins where he knew places that would particularly seek after and value them.

He wrote that he felt it best, he said, to offer to take the whole collection, and he was very happy to have them in one lot rather than split them up. If I was agreeable, he wrote, he would like to buy the whole collection for £240,000. If I would bring round the credit note, he would write a cheque for the whole amount.

****

I read the letter through several times. Because it was on such flimsy paper and poorly folded, I sandwiched the letter between two other pieces of more robust paper and tucked it into my Savings Book together with my credit note. I would take it along with my Student Identification Cards. I blessed Mrs Clarke for providing one with my father's name tacked on to the end as well as the one with the Kingswell name only as surname.

For I would get the old man in the Gold Mart to write the cheque out to Tony, and I planned to take the cheque with me and ask Tony to walk with me to his bank so we could pay it into his account.

It was beyond coincidence that the two amounts were the same—the amount that Tony and Pat had lent their son to try to help him in his hour of need, and the value of the coins in the larger of the two metal boxes. My father was either a magician or a very clever man. I had always known my father was clever. I was proud that my father had trusted me to have the courage to go and retrieve the boxes and carry out the tasks.

****

I cycled round to Charing Cross Road and propped my bike at the curb. Soon I would need to return the bike to Darren and buy a bike for myself, as Mrs Robinson had recommended.

There was someone already in the shop, so I went back outside and took time to padlock the bike up and wait a bit. I rang the doorbell for entry. The old feller peered at me, and I briefly showed him the credit note. He nodded acknowledgement and gave me a great smile, the area within his beard opening up to show irregular nicotine-stained teeth. He indicated that I should sit on the chair in the corner of the shop and wait while he attended to the other customer.

I was fascinated to see the transaction going on—a to-ing and a fro-ing. A hesitation. It took some time. Finally, agreement was reached. The customer left, turning away and shielding his face.

Now it was my turn.

I put the credit note on the counter between us, and the old man picked it up with his gnarled fingers and inspected it, then anchored it to the counter with a solid nugget. I held out the flimsy letter that he had sent and confirmed that I wanted to sell the whole collection.

'Was there any one coin amongst them all that you wanted to keep?'

I shook my head.

'It's a pleasure to do business with you,' he said.

There was no sign of the metal box. Nor the coins.

I produced my Identification Cards. He peered at them both.

'I have two surnames,' I said. 'But they're both me.'

'It's often the case,' he said. 'Which one would you like the cheque made out to?'

I pointed to the one which ended with my father's name. 'But no initial,' I said. 'Or only Tony. I'm paying it into the account of my father's father.'

He had the cheque with the amount already made out. Such amounts seemed to be everyday business to him. He had a croaky voice, and it was difficult to make out exactly what he was saying, but I gathered he was aware of their provenance now, as he called it, and was able to marry it up with other deposits. He added Tony's name. He gave me the cheque and a receipt for the coins.

'Did you want the metal box?' he croaked. 'I'm not sure where I've put it. But I could probably find it.'

I thought on reflection that it would only add complications. I thought not.

'Once again, it's a pleasure to do business with you.'

'Thank you very much,' I said.

I put away my two Identification Student Cards, the cheque and the letter.

'Thank you.'

****

I wasted no time and cycled round to Tony and Pat's again. I always thought of them as a pair, though Pat was long gone.

It was mid-morning, and Tony was sitting in the lounge in his shirt sleeves, reading yesterday's newspaper. His neighbour passed the paper on to him each day, he said, when he had finished reading it—a day late.

'Tony, I want to walk with you round to your bank and pay a cheque in. If you can put your jacket on, let's get it done.'

He folded the newspaper and laid it down on the arm of the chair. 'Never say no to a bit going in. Hang on a jiffy. I've got a Paying-In Book somewhere.'

Only Tony would use a paying-in book, I thought.

I said, 'Tony, they would always give you a loose slip to fill in.'

But, being Tony, he preferred to follow his customary practice and, sure enough, he found his Paying-In Book.

We stood at the counter in the bank, and Tony carefully filled in the date at the top. Then he glanced over to the cheque I was holding to read the numbers and copy them onto the slip in his Paying-In Book. His eyes fixed on the enormous amount. He didn't falter— just copied them in.

'I hope you've got the commas and the dots in the right place,' I said.

'I hope you're going to explain later,' he said.

I checked that it was all in order. Tony handed it in through the grill—cheque and Paying-In Book—and waited to get his book stamped and handed back.

'It will take three days to arrive in the account,' the bank teller announced.

****

My explanation to him was the barest outline of what had transpired—a bowdlerised version of the events. By the end of it, Tony understood that somehow his and Pat's loan had been repaid. He was grateful. It would take him time, but slowly he would get back on an even keel.

I assured him that I would look in on him each exeat or holiday. He asked if I would accompany him sometime in the future to visit his son in prison. I told him that I was not sure whether I needed to visit my father again, but I would try to organise it for him to go.

The outcome was the sort of thing, I thought, that only happened in books or films.

****

Looking back, I knew that, as I had lain in my sleeping bag in Lincoln's Inn Fields, a homeless with nowhere to go, looking up at the stars in the night sky, I had made an inspired choice on writing the letter to Grandfather Kingswell with my petition to ask to stay

277

in his house. Like a pebble cast into a pond, the ripples had spread in many directions. It had worked out well.

THE END